Winter's Tales

NEW SERIES 8

Winter's Tales

NEW SERIES: 8

*

EDITED BY

Robin Baird-Smith

St. Martin's Press
New York

Library of Congress catalogue card number: 89–62382

ISBN 0–312–08922–8

First U.S. Edition: February 1993
10 9 8 7 6 5 4 3 2 1

CONTENTS

ACKNOWLEDGEMENTS

The stories are copyrights respectively
© 1992 Muriel Spark
© 1992 Peter Goldsworthy
© 1992 Monica Furlong
© 1992 Juan Forn
© 1992 Angela Huth
© 1992 Chaim Potok
© 1992 Will Self
© 1992 Tony Peake
© 1992 Shelley Weiner
© 1992 Laura Kalpakian
© 1992 Richard Austin

The right of the above to be
identified as the authors of their works
has been asserted by them in accordance
with the Copyrights Designs and Patents Act 1988

EDITOR'S NOTE

To open almost any collection of short stories is to start on a journey. Familiar aspects of the landscape are bathed in light which makes one look at them anew – paths lead into unknown territory. Everywhere there is the excitement of the unexpected, the exciting contrasts of the unfolding scene.

This is certainly true of this year's *Winter's tales*. Not only are the authors drawn from a number of different countries and traditions; the ancient metaphor of the journey also holds, for this edition of *Winter's tales* traverses the ages of man. From the cruelty of youth – Will Self's 'The Indian Mutiny', the desperation of adolescent love – Monica Furlong's 'Carla, Cara' – through the boisterous prime of life to middle age, old age – Shelley Weiner's 'The Picture' – each one of these stories both tellingly encapsulates human emotion and focusses a fragment of the timespan of our lives – and our hereafter. Muriel Spark's brilliant 'The Girl I Left Behind Me', Juan Forn's 'Swimming in the Dark' and Richard Austin's 'Sister Monica's Last Journey' all enter this realm, and illustrate the great strength of this collection, for these stories, witty, perfectly crafted, all equally compelling, are yet totally different in style and feeling.

If the end of life is a strong theme, it is presented here as an element of life itself, a stage of the journey which is only a part of the cycle of human experience, glorious, funny, sad, which the stories celebrate. Each of the writers represented entertain but also, widely different as they are, they both display the craft of the story teller at its best and broaden our horizons. They present insights which irradiate not only their stories but our view of humanity.

Robin Baird-Smith

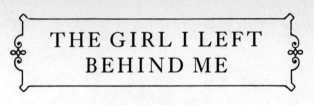

THE GIRL I LEFT BEHIND ME

Muriel Spark

It was just gone quarter past six when I left the office.

'Teedle-um-tum-tum' – there was the tune again, going round my head. Mr Letter had been whistling it all throughout the day between his noisy telephone calls and his dreamy sessions. Sometimes he whistled 'Softly, Softly, Turn the Key', but usually it was 'The Girl I Left Behind Me' rendered at a brisk hornpipe tempo.

I stood in the bus queue, tired out, and wondering how long I would endure Mark Letter (Screws & Nails) Ltd. Of course, after my long illness, it was experience. But Mr Letter and his tune, and his sudden moods of bounce, and his sudden lapses into lassitude, his sandy hair and little bad teeth, roused my resentment, especially when his tune barrelled round my head long after I had left the office; it was like taking Mr Letter home.

No one at the bus stop took any notice of me. Well, of course, why should they? I was not acquainted with anyone there, but that evening I felt particularly anonymous among the home-goers. Everyone looked right through me and even, it seemed, walked through me. Late autumn always sets my fancy towards sad ideas. The starlings were crowding in to roost on all the high cornices of the great office buildings. And I located, amongst the misty unease of my feelings, a very strong conviction that I had left something important behind me or some job incompleted at the office. Perhaps I had left the safe unlocked, or perhaps it was something quite trivial which nagged at me. I had half a mind to turn back, tired as I was, and reassure myself. But my bus came along and I piled in with the rest.

As usual, I did not get a seat. I clung to the handrail and allowed myself to be lurched back and forth against the other passengers. I stood on a man's foot, and said, 'Oh sorry.' But he looked away without response, which depressed me. And more and more, I felt that I had left something of tremendous import at the office. 'Teedle-um-tum-tum' – the tune was a background to my worry all the way home. I went over in my mind the day's business, for I thought, now, perhaps it was a letter which I should have written and posted on my way home.

That morning I had arrived at the office to find Mark Letter vigorously at work. By fits, he would occasionally turn up at eight in the morning, tear at the post and, by the time I arrived, he would have despatched perhaps half a dozen needless telegrams; and before I could get my coat off, would deliver a whole day's instructions to me, rapidly fluttering his freckled hands in time with his chattering mouth. This habit used to jar me, and I found only one thing amusing about it; that was when he would say, as he gave instructions for dealing with each item, 'Mark letter urgent.' I thought that rather funny coming from Mark Letter, and I often thought of him, as he was in those moods, as Mark Letter Urgent.

As I swayed in the bus I recalled that morning's access of energy on the part of Mark Letter Urgent. He had been more urgent than usual, so that I still felt put out by the urgency. I felt terribly old for my twenty-two years as I raked round my mind for some clue as to what I had left unfinished. Something had been left amiss; the further the bus carried me from the office, the more certain I became of it. Not that I took my job to heart very greatly, but Mr Letter's moods of bustle were infectious, and when they occurred I felt fussy for the rest of the day; and although I consoled myself that I would feel better when I got home, the worry would not leave me.

By noon, Mr Letter had calmed down a little, and for an hour before I went to lunch he strode round the office with his hands in his pockets, whistling between his seedy brown teeth that sailors' song 'The Girl I Left Behind Me'. I lurched with the bus as it chugged out the rhythm, 'Teedle-um-tum-tum. Teedle-um . . .' Returning from lunch I had found silence, and wondered if Mr Letter was out, until I heard suddenly, from his tiny private office, his tune again, a low swift hum, trailing out towards the end. Then I knew that he had fallen into one of his afternoon daydreams.

I would sometimes come upon him in his little box of an office when these trances afflicted him. I would find him sitting in his swivel chair behind his desk. Usually he had taken off his coat and slung it across the back of his chair. His right elbow would be propped on the desk, supporting his chin, while from his left hand would dangle his tie. He would gaze at this tie; it was his main object of contemplation. That afternoon I had found him tie-gazing when I went into his room for some papers. He was gazing at it with parted lips so that I could see his small, separated discoloured teeth, no larger than a child's first teeth. Through them he whistled his tune. Yesterday, it had been 'Softly, Softly, Turn the Key', but today it was the other.

I got off the bus at my usual stop, with my fare still in my hand. I almost threw the coins away, absentmindedly thinking they were the ticket, and when I noticed them I thought how nearly no one at all I was, since even the conductor had, in his rush, passed me by.

Mark Letter had remained in his dream for two and a half hours. What was it I had left unfinished? I could not for the life of me recall what he had said when at last he emerged from his office-box. Perhaps it was then I had made tea. Mr Letter always liked a cup when he was neither in his frenzy nor in his abstraction, but ordinary and talkative. He would speak of his hobby, fretwork. I do not think Mr Letter had any home life. At forty-six he was still unmarried, living alone in a house at

Roehampton. As I walked up the lane to my lodgings I recollected that Mr Letter had come in for his tea with his tie still dangling from his hand, his throat white under the open-neck shirt, and his 'Teedle-um-tum-tum' in his teeth.

At last I was home and my Yale in the lock. Softly, I said to myself, softly turn the key, and thank God I'm home. My landlady passed through the hall from kitchen to dining-room with a salt and pepper cruet in her crinkly hands. She had some new lodgers. 'My guests', she always called them. The new guests took precedence over the old with my landlady. I felt desolate. I simply could not climb the stairs to my room to wash, and then descend to take brown soup with the new guests while my landlady fussed over them, ignoring me. I sat for a moment in the chair in the hall to collect my strength. A year's illness drains one, however young. Suddenly the repulsion of the brown soup and the anxiety about the office made me decide. I would not go upstairs to my room. I must return to the office to see what it was that I had overlooked.

'Teedle-um-tum-tum' – I told myself that I was giving way to neurosis. Many times I had laughed at my sister who, after she had gone to bed at night, would send her husband downstairs to make sure all the gas taps were turned off, all the doors locked, back and front. Very well, I was as silly as my sister, but I understood her obsession, and simply opened the door and slipped out of the house, tired as I was, making my weary way back to the bus stop, back to the office.

'Why should I do this for Mark Letter?' I demanded of myself. But really, I was not returning for his sake, it was for my own. I was doing this to get rid of the feeling of incompletion, and that song in my brain swimming round like a damned goldfish.

I wondered, as the bus took me back along the familiar route, what I would say if Mark Letter should still be at the office. He often worked late, or at least, stayed there late, doing I don't know what, for his screw and nail business did not call for long hours. It seemed to me he had an affection for those dingy premises. I was rather apprehensive lest I should find Mr Letter at the office, standing, just as I had last seen him, swinging his tie in his hand, beside my desk. I resolved that if I should find him there, I should say straight out that I had left something behind me.

A clock struck quarter past seven as I got off the bus. I realized that again I had not paid my fare. I looked at the money in my hand for a stupid second. Then I felt reckless. 'Teedle-um-tum-tum' – I caught myself humming the tune as I walked quickly up the sad side-street to our office. My heart knocked at my throat, for I was eager. Softly, softly, I said to myself as I turned the key of the outside door. Quickly, quickly, I ran up the stairs. Only outside the office door I halted, and while I found its key on my bunch it occurred to me how strangely my sister would think I was behaving.

I opened the door and my sadness left me at once. With a great joy I recognized what it was I had left behind me, my body lying strangled on the floor. I ran towards my body and embraced it like a lover.

THE DEATH OF DAFFY DUCK

Peter Goldsworthy

The two couples had eaten together once a month since their university days; eaten their way through the menus of most of the decent restaurants around town, and more than a few of the indecent. At times others shared their table – other couples, the odd 'confirmed bachelor' friend or visiting relative – but the booking was usually a Table For Four.

Things had gone well over the years for all four friends, professionally. Terry Hicks had established himself as one of the younger, and braver, bone surgeons in the city; his wife Mary – Mary Barratt, one of the first of her generation to keep her maiden name – taught architecture at the Institute. Scott and Jenny Greaves were both lawyers – Scott working in the Crown Law Department, Jenny in private, dealing with Family Law briefs mainly.

Neither couple had yet produced children, although the time for final decisions was fast approaching; the women were both in their mid-thirties, and at times, especially late at night – alone with themselves, isolated from the snug, sleeping world that surrounded them by insomnia – both felt a little anxious. Their various mothers and fathers and mothers-in-law had long ago dropped the subject, but both women retained a half-conscious understanding that yes, they *would* one day have children, even if they denied the wish in public.

Meanwhile, there was still fun to be had, childless freedom to enjoy. The monthly dinners were riotous affairs; money was thrown about as loosely as talk, course followed course, imported liqueurs followed imported wines, the tips at the end of the night were uniformly big irrespective of service. Mary –

the architect – had a penchant for desserts. Her meal often consisted of nothing but an entrée, followed by three different rich desserts; yet somehow she maintained the trimmest figure. *Too* trim, her friend Jenny privately thought – although in public Jenny always expressed mock-chagrin at the quantities of food Mary permitted herself. In their school-days together Jenny had been the ugly one, tagging along in Mary's wake; now she felt more equal, was *made* to feel more equal, even, or especially, by the men. Clothes of most kinds still hung best on Mary – but in a swimming pool, or naked before a mirror, Jenny was fully aware of who was more womanly in shape and volume. She was careful to keep her shape that way, and no more, sticking to small picky seafood portions, salads, fruit platters.

It was often Jenny's insistence that led to the choice of restaurant: *nouvelle cuisine*, Thai, even once a vegetarian place.

The bill was rotated between the couples, though if someone forgot their wallet or purse, or paid out of turn, no one worried – money seemed plentiful, generosity was a virtue that all four could easily afford.

At the birthday dinners – four a year – extravagant gifts changed hands: imported perfumes, cameras, wines, electronic toys. Spending on *any*thing, for its own sake, was a form of generosity, Scott – Deputy Crown Prosecutor at thirty-five – proclaimed on one such occasion. Small, wiry, quick with his tongue, he liked to harangue his friends as if they were jurors. There was nothing *wrong* with conspicuous consumption, he pronounced – as long as the money was spent quickly enough.

'The *velocity* of money is what matters, not the amount. You have to keep the money moving. If everyone spends quickly enough, everyone can take turns being a millionaire.'

'Briefly,' his wife quibbled.

'Does that matter? You still get to *spend* the money.'

[20]

There had been occasional hiccups in the relationship; in particular one upper-case Scene involving a smashed glass between the men. Scott was one of those whose dislikes were stronger than his likes; he was at his most passionate on things he detested, especially bad wine. Wine was his area of expertise; Terry had chosen from the wine list without consulting him; an absurd argument over degrees of dryness had followed, the smallest of disagreements, as always, provoking the most heated clash.

The second dispute was a little more serious. Terry had a kind of Daffy Duck voice that he often slipped into, especially late at night, or when drunk: a voice that let things slip that were too embarrassing or too serious to speak of in normal conversation; a voice that could say things from behind a duck-mask, with a fool's frankness. The voice had quacked out its lust for Jenny, his wife's friend, once too often, the truth half-hidden under cover of banter, but this time not sufficiently; the silence that followed revealed something about themselves to each of the four.

That silence seemed to last for minutes. Finally one of two things had to happen: someone had to say, yes, let's do it, let's *swap*, or someone had to say, I think that's enough, you've spoiled the evening. It could have gone either way; Mary chose the latter, reining her husband in.

After the paying of that particular bill, there had been no dinner for several months. And yet even lust for another's spouse was forgivable, and finally easily forgivable; forgiveness was another virtue all four could easily afford.

And the subject was now dead. Despite the odd thigh-rub beneath the table things had developed no further; all four were contented in their marriages; contented enough, at any rate, to prefer the ease and familiarity of friendship to the disturbances and unpredictability of lust.

It was the third Scene which proved irreparable.

Scott and Terry had always been competitors to some extent. Their friendship had grown through the two women, old school friends; when the men first met, at university, there had been a long period of verbal jostling, a friendly rivalry that had now settled into a weekly round of highly competitive golf. The dinners usually organized themselves after a Saturday round; or after the 'girls' bridge night' which Mary and Jenny attended within a larger circle of their old school friends on alternate Thursday nights.

Terry had been an athlete, solid and muscular at school; the good life had filled that athleticism out, it was now a little overfed, reddish-skinned, lumpen. His shirt-collars were too tight on his plump neck; his face had coarsened. He was known in the hospitals as an athletic surgeon, prone to all-night marathons, or record-time joint replacements – a Hero, in the parlance. No intellectual, or diagnostician, he had always enjoyed most the hands-on stuff, the sawing, drilling, cutting. He revelled in massive road trauma: multiple injuries, quick decision-making, actual *physical* challenges.

He always ate red meat. He always drank heavily. He often spoke with his mouth full, it seemed to help his Daffy Duck voice. And once – in a crowded Greek taverna – he breathed in as he spoke.

This also seemed to be a performance at first: a duck-spluttery cry for help.

'Gone down the wrong way?' Mary asked, good-humouredly, as he began to cough.

Jenny reached over to pat his back – but he had already run out of air to cough with, the cough was swallowed by a strangled sound and suddenly he was on his feet, reared up, something large and red-faced breaching above the surface of seated diners. His gagging was framed in a total, sudden silence; then people at nearby tables began shouting:

'He's choking!'

'Christ! Somebody help him.'

'Ring an ambulance!'

His face was purpling; he seemed to be trying to say something – perhaps how to help him – but no sound emerged, there was no breath to fill out the words. He took a single step back, then fell forward on to the table in a clatter of glass and cutlery, ripping at his collar and tie.

'Is there a doctor here?' a waiter screamed above the shouting diners, but the only doctor seemed to be choking to death, among broken glass and spilled wine, on a table-top.

It took Scott – usually so quick in court, so decisive, at least with his tongue – some time to react. Or to realize what was happening. Somehow he knew what to do – seizing his bigger friend from behind, balling both his fists in the solar plexus, jerking up and back with all his strength. Something seemed to give, a loosened plug; Terry rolled on to his side on the wrecked table, a stream of vomit was coughed out on to the floor, he began wheezing, making great sucking sounds, still panic-stricken. Scott forced a finger into his friend's mouth, searching for any further blockage, and was rewarded with a bite. He withdrew his finger with a shout of pain, bleeding heavily.

The ambulance arrived, a stretcher was wheeled in, but Terry was already recovering. He recognized the ambulance officers, and refused abruptly to go with them, sitting off to one side of the table, dropping his head down in his hands, still wheezing.

'That might need a couple of stitches,' an ambulance officer murmured to Scott, and flipped open a first-aid box, and wrapped the bleeding, bitten finger in an oily gauze.

'I'll be fine,' Scott murmured, some part of him not wanting to steal the scene from his friend.

He sat down again at the table with Terry and the two women. Around them the restaurant was returning to normal

[23]

status. Their tablecloth was deftly whipped away with all food, cutlery, plates and vomit wrapped inside it; a fresh cloth was flung casually across the table, drinks and place-settings materialized.

No one seemed able to speak, and at length Terry rose, peeled off a couple of large-denomination notes from his wallet, and walked out of the restaurant.

Mary sat for another thirty seconds or so, then rose also.

'Perhaps I'd better leave too.'

'Of course,' Jenny murmured.

And so they parted, four people who had never, until that moment, asked a single question of the world; had never had reason to. They were innocents, insulated from the kinds of pain that had goaded lesser minds than theirs into better lives than theirs; there had been no real mysteries.

Terry failed to appear at the golf club the following Saturday morning; Scott made up a foursome with some old school friends after waiting an hour at the clubhouse bar. In the afternoon he left a brief, cheerful message on his friend's answering machine, but some sixth sense warned him not to press further; especially when on a Saturday morning a fortnight later, as he was chipping on to the eighteenth green, he saw Terry on a distant fairway with a couple of total strangers.

Jenny reported home after a bridge night that Mary had merely mentioned that Terry was 'busy', avoiding any further discussion. Mary herself rang Scott after a month; her voice was steady as she explained that Terry didn't 'feel up to facing you right now'.

'But I would like to thank you for what you did,' she said. 'Who knows – it might have been serious.'

Scott took some umbrage at this; as did Jenny when he replayed the conversation to her. Her years as a teenage ugly-duckling had given her a sharp sense of injustice.

'It might have been *serious*?' she said, in a voice as near to a shout as she ever came. 'You saved his life! Don't they *know* that?'

She planned to make that very point to Mary at the next bridge night, but Mary didn't show; someone's husband was required to stand in at short notice to make up the numbers. The same husband was required again the following fortnight, and the fortnight after that a new member was found to join the circle, permanently.

There were no more restaurant Tables for Four; Jenny's birthday brought a card from Mary, and a brief note – *Snowed under with work, hope to catch up with you soon* – which both Scott and Jenny were now able to recognize meant exactly the opposite.

In the small, closed universe of Adelaide, of course, all paths intersect sooner or later. Once, Scott thought he saw Terry cross to the other side of the Mall, and vanish into a shop as he approached. But there could be no crossing the street when the two men came face to face in a corridor a year later.

'Terry – how are you?'

'Never been better.'

Scott had halted, but Terry was still moving, almost past him. Scott wanted to reach out and restrain his friend, but hesitated too long. As Terry walked away, he decided to break the ice, turn the taboo subject into a joke, defuse it with humour. Perhaps once it was out in the open, the problem would be gone.

'Last time I saw you you didn't look so good,' he said.

Terry stopped, and turned. His face seemed genuinely puzzled. 'Must have been a long time back, Scott.'

And he walked on, leaving Scott standing, flatfooted; but after ten paces he turned yet again, and this time shouted, his face purple with anger, as purple as it had been on the night of the Scene:

'What do you want – a fucking medal?'

The words came in a shower of duck-spittle; then he turned on his heel and walked quickly away, and they would never speak again.

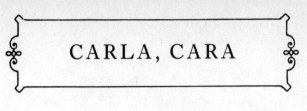

CARLA, CARA

Monica Furlong

It was the summer of 1939 and the two of them ate out of doors in the little café in the park, Carla having dutifully shown Franz the Zoo. When they had finished their meal Carla did something he never forgot. She picked up the mustard pot, unscrewed it and then put a generous dollop of the stuff in the bottom of her teacup which was still half full of tea. She added generous shakes of salt and pepper, some tomato sauce, then some hot water from the jug. She stirred the mixture vigorously, then pushed it towards her cousin.

'If you love me, drink that!' she said, and Franz did drink it, unhesitatingly, in one appalling gulp, his pale spotted face flushing with emotion.

'So!' she said, as if something was settled or understood between them, as in fact it was. Franz gave a small modest smile.

He had arrived in England three weeks before on a children's transport, exhausted and staring like a sleepwalker. He ate like a starving man, went to bed and slept for hours. (He did not tell his uncle and aunt how the children had been promised food as soon as they arrived on the English coast. The Women's Institute had wheeled a trolley full of soup and rolls on to the platform and the hungry children had had to turn politely away or throw their portions into the fire buckets. The soup had pieces of ham floating in it, and the sandwiches were full of bacon. It would be the first of many misunderstandings from well-meaning hosts. He also did not tell them of the last painful glimpse of his mother who, alone among the parents, had broken through the barrier behind which they were confined, and run along the platform to where Franz was craning his head from a window. For the rest of his life he never mentioned that image to anyone.)

But on the interminable journey Franz knew that he was lucky in that he was going to relatives, and that he even knew Uncle Ernst, who had made many business trips to Berlin. Once arrived, though, he lay in bed summoning up the smell of home, the taste of sauerkraut, the sound of his mother rattling saucepans in the kitchen, the peppery smell of the geraniums on the balcony, the feel of the piano, of the shiny saddle of his bike. He knew he was going to die of homesickness.

'What a chance to improve your English!' his mother had said, she who would have declared hell itself a broadening experience if she thought it would make him feel better. He had long ago given up telling her his troubles, which had multiplied for months.

He did not expect much of life with Uncle Ernst and Aunt Ruthie, still less of the famous boys' school to which he was going to be sent, guessing the fate of those who were foreigners and worse than foreigners. His German pride resented the miserable status of the refugee – 'you know about him, poor boy – goodness knows what will happen to his parents' – and his youth resented the pit of sadness into which he was plunged.

As he finished his long sleep, and tried to summon the courage to get up and begin his new life in England, he recognized there was one thing he had not calculated for – his cousin Carla. As he had stumbled out of the train at Victoria, too shy to know how tired he was, the first thing that caught his eye, standing alongside Uncle Ernst and Aunt Ruthie, was this stunningly pretty girl, maybe a year or two older than himself. She stared back, and giggled. She had curling black hair that swung around her slim waist and she was wearing a pink dress the colour of sugar almonds. She had eyes which, extraordinarily, were navy blue, with wonderful clear whites to them, a face that it was difficult not to stare at. Aunt Ruthie enclosed him in a warm hug which he would have enjoyed more if he was not so intoxicated with Carla. He, who knew no girls, was going to live under a roof with this one.

Carla's response was less enthusiastic.

'Mother, he's ghastly!' she said when Franz had gone to bed to get over his journey. Franz was plump and pale, with an unlovely scattering of adolescent spots. He seemed almost entirely silent. He exuded tiredness, sorrow, despair.

'He'll be better when he's settled down,' said her mother. 'Remember what he's gone through. I think you should try to be like a sister to him. He's never had a sister, nor you a brother, and it will be good for you both.'

Carla groaned. She could see it all. She would have to conduct this mournful exile to Buckingham Palace and the Tower, and God knew where. She began curling the hair upwards from her forehead in a huge puff the way the Hollywood stars were wearing it.

'That'll never fit under your school hat,' said her mother.

Just as Carla had feared, she and Franz had almost nothing in common. To her disgust he enjoyed things she dismissed as boring – the pictures in the National Gallery, for instance.

'You mean you do not like such pictures?' he asked her wonderingly, as he gazed at the Rembrandts. He was always fiddling the wireless to find classical music, or asking her which was her favourite Shakespeare play – his was *Macbeth* – and he was surprised to find that she only really liked Hollywood films and funny programmes on the wireless, and that she thought Shakespeare was a crashing bore.

'We're doing *A Midsummer Night's Dream* this term. Well, it's silly, isn't it, all fairies. Nobody believes in fairies.'

When she took him to Hollywood films he, in his turn,

thought they were silly, especially if there was a lot of dancing in them.

'People do not live like that, so romantic, such lovely houses.'

Yet the two of them were bound together by youth, by the necessity of living in the same house and by Aunt Ruthie's rules of hospitality. Also, although largely indifferent to world events, Carla heard enough at synagogue to grasp a little of the plight of Franz and his parents.

'If there is a war he won't even be able to write to his parents, will he?' she asked her mother. Carla could not even imagine a life without indulgent parents constantly present. 'Poor old Franz.'

She was irritated by Franz's punctilious German ways, and his careful application to English. ('Don't ask *me*,' she would say pettishly if he asked her for help with his vocabulary.) She was more than irritated by his highbrow tastes, but she was moved by her pity for him, and perhaps by something else – something dogged, amused, shrewd, that gleamed through the homesickness and the uncertainties. Unexpectedly he was good at table tennis. He was ruthless in his attempt to win, but seemed quite pleased when she sometimes beat him. He had a kind of wit in his strokes, too, as if playing the game was a pleasing art in which finesse was more fun than brutal winning techniques. Alert, excited, giving brief shouts of triumph, he was a different boy from the pale scholar struggling to get his grammar right.

More interesting than this, though, was that she saw she had a startling effect on Franz. She was already used to attracting male attention. A boy from the grammar school used to hang round school in the hope of riding home with her on the bus, and there had been boys at the few dances Uncle Ernst allowed her to go to who had tried to get her to go out with them (which she would have done if allowed), but she knew of no other boy who coloured to the tips of his ears when she looked at him, who gazed at her like one possessed over the cornflakes, that found a beautiful Pre-Raphaelite in the Tate and brought home a postcard of it murmuring, 'That is like you.' Without being at all in love with Franz, Carla was captivated by his fascination with her, and could not hear enough of his compliments, though Franz was understandably shy about elaborating.

Waking and sleeping, he had begun to dream of Carla. Just as if she was a product of the Hollywood dream factory, Carla was, for Franz, a talisman warding off terror and grief and hatred and loss, and in particular that last glimpse of his mother. There was something about Carla that was merry and wholesome, as well as young and beautiful, and he supped it up with gratitude. Alone in his room, he liked to repeat her name to himself, sentimentally adding the word 'cara'. 'Carla, cara' became a silent prayer against homesickness, despair, bullying. With her in his mind he could endure anything. So that when Carla, with her own native wit, handed him the potion in the teacup, it was a pleasure to drink the fiery liquid and declare his faith.

'Would you like to kiss me?' Carla asked curiously. Franz blushed, and nodded, and later, on a seat overlooking the lake, he did kiss her. He kissed briefly and shyly, but with tenderness.

'You've never kissed a girl before, have you?' Carla asked. That was of course true, though, lacking other opportunities, he had surreptitiously practised on a few female relatives, sometimes surprising elderly aunts by kissing them warmly on the lips. He would have liked to have continued the experiment with this more congenial companion but she got up and walked on. She had got more of a thrill than she had expected from forcing him to drink the fiery draught. In her fantasy it had been a sort of love-potion with herself as the witch binding him to her power, but then it was clear immediately that he was in love already, and scarcely needed potions. Maybe it was more of a test, or ordeal, a task set to prove his faithfulness. Suddenly drunk with power, it occurred to Carla that she might submit Franz to a series of tests, each suitably rewarded, to see how much he cared.

The first of these was that, at synagogue on Saturday, he should give a loud cry. It occurred to her that, because Franz was so much the perfect child in her parents' eyes – studious, obedient, dutiful – she wanted to see him get into trouble. From the gallery where she sat she could not see Franz, but suddenly from below there was a wailing, strangled cry, followed by some exclamations and a sound of people moving and hurrying that she could not quite place. Had they thrown him out, or what? She and the other women looked at one another in surprise. Later her father explained.

'The poor boy came over faint. The first we knew of it he gave this sort of scream and keeled over. Makes you realize more of what he's gone through.' Franz listened to all this from the sofa, where he did look paler than usual. When her mother and father had left the room he grinned at Carla.

'Five minutes of kissing,' he reminded her. 'When?'

Carla enjoyed Franz's kissing more than she had expected and quickly thought up another torment.

'Eat a piece of fried bacon,' she suggested. 'I can get a piece off Jenny and cook it when Mum is out at bridge.'

'No!' said Franz.

'Not to feel inside my blouse?' she tempted him.

Without even pausing to consider the bait that was being offered, Franz said indignantly, 'I never would. And while we are about it don't ever ask me to do anything that hurts anyone either.'

'That's not the same thing at all,' said Carla defensively.

'It is to me.'

For the first time in their acquaintance she felt discomfited. She tossed her head. 'You've lost your chance now,' she said.

'No more privileges.' But she was enjoying the game too much to stop, so they invented a new bargain. Franz failed a school exam in his very best subject – mathematics – in order to undo the buttons of Carla's blouse.

'How will I know you have done it?' she asked.

'You have my word,' said Franz stiffly, and went ahead deliberately to get the answers wrong. Even then, he only just failed.

A very disappointing exam result, Mr Meredew wrote on his report, but Franz thought it was well worth it. Jenny, Carla's best friend, thought it was shameful when Carla told her about it.

'Poor boy, why are you so rotten to him?'

'Because he's fat, and got spots, and is so sort of ...' Carla could not think of a word to describe what she despised about him.

'I think he is really nice,' said Jenny, who had a kind heart. But she wasn't so pretty as Carla.

For his part, Franz had no sense of grievance. It seemed to him natural enough that he should have to earn the privileges Carla offered, and he was prepared to live contentedly in the memory of them and in anticipation of new ones to come. Being naturally law-abiding he took an odd sort of pleasure in the glint of danger that now hung over his life, so different from the blind anger and despair of the recent past. He told Carla to himself like a Catholic telling his beads. 'Carla, cara!' he said, alone in his room, over and over again, something he did not dare to say to her when he touched her.

Carla was surprised to find that she enjoyed Franz's kisses more than she had expected. He kissed gently, gracefully, where the other few boys who had tried had been rough and clumsy. When he undid her blouse, and cupped her small breast in his hand the expression on his face as he looked down at it was one of tenderness, and he stroked it like silk. This moved her. But she was equally moved by her consciousness of her power over Franz – that he would take risks for her, do her bidding. The thought excited her, with a sudden, quick spasm deep in her gut.

The summer holidays came and Carla and Franz were sent to the country to stay with relatives in Berkshire, who bred horses. Freed of school and homework they walked and swam in a local lake. They tried to learn to ride on a couple of old hacks, they helped in the work with the horses, they picked blackcurrants and raspberries, and made lemonade to drink on the hot afternoons beneath the trees. Franz grew brown, perhaps for the first time in his life, and he was taller and thinner. Carla took photographs of him for him to send home to his mother. They found an old tree house that had belonged to a long-gone gaggle of children, and had fun making it their own. On the radio there was talk of war.

Once, in the cool shadow of the stable, when the horses were out riding, Franz tried again to kiss Carla, but she pushed him away.

'Not now!' she said. 'Soon!'

It was on a day of swimming and picnicking that, walking home through the woods, they came to the place where the railway cut through between modest banks. There was a level crossing where the rails were embedded in a wooden floor, and a gate each side which just allowed room for one person to stand beside the track. It was not far to the bend where the train would come steaming round the corner and bear down upon the level crossing.

'I will take off my clothes in the wood and let you kiss me if you will accept a dare,' said Carla.

'What dare?' said Franz, suddenly alert.

'You will lie down on the track and I will tie you to it with my scarf. I will stand up on the bank where I can see exactly where the train is, and when I tell you, though not a second before, you will untie the scarf and get off the track.'

'OK,' said Franz, who had recently adopted this expression with its cool American neutrality. He said it so promptly that she felt disappointed, then wondered if he had understood.

'You mustn't move a finger until I tell you to.'

'OK,' said Franz again.

'Aren't you nervous?'

Franz did not reply, simply looked at her and laughed. Then he said, as a statement, not a question, 'In the wood. *All* your clothes.'

She felt a little cheated – she had counted on seeing Franz hesitate – but she pulled off the scarf, as they crouched on the wooden platform, and tied it around the rail and then around Franz's waist. She used a double knot.

She sat and talked to him for a bit, then left him and went and stood up on the bank. She could not hear Franz muttering over and over to himself, 'Carla, cara, Carla, cara,' and trying to prevent his fingers from automatically moving to the knot of the scarf. Yet he knew that this new person he had become, this new person Carla had made him, had more life and joy in him than the good Jewish boy at home. How appalled his mother would be if she could see him.

He could feel the vibration of the train, far off but moving towards him, the song of the wheels along the tracks, a whistle, a sound of discharged steam. Now he had to hold his hand consciously in place, sure that Carla must be watching his every movement. Because the sun was in his eyes he could not see Carla but she called to him several times, 'Not long now. It's round the next bend.' He suddenly knew that he was terribly frightened, lying there like a sacrifice, and that he would not quite put it past Carla to let the worst happen. He made an extraordinary resolve for a fourteen-year-old boy, that if he had to die he would offer his life joyfully for Carla. 'Carla, cara,' he murmured again.

The ground jarred indescribably, shaking him all over, and Carla cried, 'Now!' Without thought he pulled at the scarf, which terrified him by a moment's resistance (Carla had tied the knot tight), got it apart, leaped off the track and stood by the gate with a few feet to spare as the huge train rushed past. He turned white beneath his tan, sickened by the huge wheels, the breath and noise and turmoil of the train. He was brusque with Carla, taking her by the arm and dragging her roughly into the thickness of the wood.

'All right!' she said, pulling herself free. When she undressed in front of him, he did not look at her with the tenderness he had shown before, but with an angry lust that humiliated her. He kissed her so hard upon the mouth that she could feel bone pressing almost intolerably against bone, and without a trace of his old shy gentleness he thrust his hand inside her. She tried to cry out but could not, and just then he pulled sharply away from her. He sat for a moment, head down, not looking at her, then stood up and walked away in the direction of the farm. Carla slowly dressed and trailed after him. By the time she got back she was of less importance to Franz than the discovery that England had declared war on Germany, and that all communication with his parents was cut off.

For a few days Franz avoided her, and she tried to read his mood. He lost interest in riding and walking and swimming and returned to his old love of reading. He said that he had a holiday assignment to finish. Carla discovered that it was difficult to amuse herself without him, that she had enjoyed his jokes and his conversation, his will to please her, his admiring glances, above all the dangerous game they had played together. She had loved this satellite which revolved around her sun and she missed it. But there was something more too. On that day on the railway track she had seen an example of courage that made it impossible to despise Franz any more. He was no longer the fat, spotty boy. In fact he was now quite slim, and much less spotty. Almost good-looking. She could not bear to think that she had lost his attention. At meals she tried to be her most winning, but he replied shortly, as if his thoughts were elsewhere.

'You must be very worried about your parents,' she said, Carla who had never mentioned his parents before. Franz snorted.

'You wouldn't know about that,' he said.

The weather was hotter than ever. Carla went for a swim, came back and looked for Franz. She guessed he might be in the barn and he was, back pressed comfortably against a pile of hay, a book unread by his side. She thought at first he was asleep, but as she crept round to look at him she saw that he was simply staring at the wall.

'Would you like to sleep with me?' she asked humbly.

'Sleep?' he said, ironically. 'Or the other thing?'

'The other thing.'

'So what's the price?'

If Carla had ever cared for other people she would have heard the scorn in his voice, but she did not notice it and went on. 'You know the narrow bit between the two barns, where the men walk across that plank sometimes to throw hay into the other hayloft? I want you to walk across it.'

Carla knew his terror of heights.

'So the game goes on,' he said. 'You sell yourself, like . . .' He did not finish the sentence but drummed with his fingers on the floor.

She had sunk down, pink from the heat, against the opposite

wall, and he looked at her as if he had never seen her before, red, alert, fierce.

'But you want me to fuck you?' He had learned this new word at school. 'So what's the point?'

Carla gave a gesture that was proud with a consciousness of her own good looks, and she looked beautiful – the smooth clear skin with the tiniest beading of sweat, the big eyes glowing in the shadow of the barn, the pretty curl and gleam of the mantle of hair.

'I will tell you. You are in love with being loved. Other people do not exist for you. It is sad. But to show you that I am not afraid . . .'

Franz stood up, a little unsteady on his legs, and began to climb the ladder to the hayloft, this time, sustained by scorn, not by his loving prayer to Carla. It was a long way from the ground, at the top of the barn, and he could see the merciless cobbled yard below him. The plank bridge between the two barns was not more than seven or eight feet yet it was an impassable canyon. His rage drove him on, out into that intolerable space where there was nothing but the barest foothold, and a mere breeze, hostile as everything natural was now hostile to him. Midway across, just as he had known would happen, all courage was gone, like a supply of oxygen or of food. His legs began to shake, ague-like, uncontrollably, betraying the body so desperate for equilibrium. He could not move, neither go forward nor back, not even sink to his knees. His shaking threw him inevitably, necessarily, without malice, out into space. As he fell he was conscious of coolness, speed, timelessness, and he thought of his mother.

'Roll just a little way to the right, young man,' said the nurse, just as if he could really move at all.

'I don't know what poor Ulrich will say when he hears,' said

Ernst, puzzled how such a quiet studious boy could manage the kind of exploit which resulted in two broken legs, a broken hip and a broken arm, never mind cuts and bruises. 'He will think I have not looked after him. Do you think the boy was trying to kill himself, perhaps?'

'Not at all,' said Ruthie. 'Have sense. No one would try to kill themselves like that, and anyway, he is so much happier than when he came – another boy altogether.'

'But the news,' said Ernst, speaking quietly although there was no one to hear. 'He knows. He is not stupid. Maybe he will never see them again.'

'I think he has tried to forget them,' said Ruthie, 'to put something else in their place.'

'His own parents!' said Ernst indignantly.

'He is only a boy. He has to survive. It was for that they sent him here.'

'It has seemed to me', said Ernst, 'that he is sweet on our Carla. Do you think so too?'

'Sweet!' said Ruthie mockingly. 'Such an old-fashioned expression.'

'But you know what I mean?'

'She has steadied down a bit just lately. Don't you think so? She offered to help me with the washing up last night.'

'I am glad. I thought she was boy-mad.'

Carla had not seen Franz in hospital; he did not want to see anyone, he said, except his uncle and aunt. She supposed he blamed her for his accident and you could scarcely wonder. She had been so afraid, sure that she had killed him, or maybe paralysed him. Just before the fall, when she had seen him standing there, so unexpectedly tall, slim, tanned, dignified, it was as if she had never seen him before and she wanted to shout out, 'Not you! I don't want you to do it. You can have me anyway.' But then pride stopped her, the thought that Franz was doing this for her like a knight of old jousting for his lady. Although he had jousted and lost she knew now that she loved him and that she would tell him so when they met – no more jousts.

Not till he was sitting up with his crutch beside him did Franz send a message that he would like to see Carla.

'Well!' she said, beginning with a touch of her old manner. 'How are things?'

Franz stared at her so hard that she began to redden. 'I have really learned something,' he said. 'That if you do something from love, as I lay down on the track, then you are miraculously preserved. If you do it out of hate, or even out of scorn, as I walked along that plank, then you invite disaster. Yes, I have learned that.'

'Did you get my card?' she asked, not certain what he was talking about, but not liking the sound of it.

'The one of Popeye with his spinach?' Franz gave a sort of barking laugh, that broke off in a spasm of pain. 'Spinach will not cure me, Carla, cara.' Now that he could use the words they were no longer a prayer.

'But you're going to be all right.'

'Oh yes, I'm going to be all right.'

'I'll make it up to you when you are better.'

'Really? Will you really?'

'I love you. *Really* love you, I mean.'

'Well, that's very nice.'

When it was time to leave Carla did her best to kiss Franz meaningfully, but he turned away. She reckoned that it was going to be hard to win this one back, but that she would treat it as a sort of challenge. On the way out she saw Jenny coming in through the hospital doors, carrying flowers and grapes and a book. She did not ask where she was going.

SWIMMING
IN THE DARK

Juan Forn

Translated from the Spanish
by Norman Thomas di Giovanni
and Susan Ashe

It was too late to be awake, especially in a borrowed house and with no lights on. Outside, in the garden, the crickets were calling out frantically for rain, and he wondered how his wife and baby daughter upstairs could sleep through the din. Plagued by insomnia, he sat in his shorts in front of the glass doors that opened on to the terrace and the lawn. The only light came from the floodlit sides of the swimming pool, and its undulating glow failed to kill the sensation of being in someone else's house, the vague unease of a pretended holiday. For, in fact, he was not there resting but working. Even though the work involved no particular effort, even though all he had to do was to live in the house with his wife and daughter, enjoying his friend Félix's possessions while he and Ruth sailed up the Nile and spent a fortune on rolls of film and toothless Egyptian guides on behalf of an Italian travel magazine.

To calm himself down, to bring on sleep, he reflected on the fact that he was not going to set foot in the city for a whole month. He would live in shorts and go without shaving, he would cut the grass, look after the pool, watch videos, and listen to Félix's CDs while his daughter grew before his eyes and his wife dreamed up exotic puddings in the kitchen. And all this time some marginally stimulating or even catastrophic message might be left on the answering machine back at his flat. Meanwhile, perhaps Félix and Ruth would extend their travels for another month or so, or have an accident, or both fall in love with the same androgynous, illiterate ephebe in Alexandria. A month away from his office could be a long time, almost a lifetime. To his little daughter, say. He must start to adapt his life to her rhythm – so his wife had told him. A day at a time, an hour at a time, slowly. Once and for all, he must get in touch with his emotions as a father – so Félix and Ruth would say if they hadn't already.

That was when he heard the door. Not the bell but two soft, polite little taps, as if in deference to the hour. Each house has its own logic, and its laws are more eloquent at night, when things take place without the soothing effect of background noise. He did not look at his watch, nor was he surprised, nor did he think the tapping was his imagination. He simply got up without turning on any light along the way, and when he opened the door he found himself face to face with his father. But his father was dead. It was only then that the son realized he had got used to the idea of never seeing his father again.

His father was wearing a raincoat buttoned up to the neck, and his hair was as thick and well groomed as ever, but completely white. Neither had ever put on much of a show of affection with the other.

'Dad, what a surprise,' the son said, but he made no move until his father asked, smiling:

'May I come in?'

'Yes, yes, of course.'

Crossing the dark living-room and going through the open glass doors, his father sat down on one of the deck chairs on the terrace. From there, he looked back into the house and, beckoning to his son, laid his hand on the empty chair by his side.

Obediently, the son stepped out on to the terrace. 'Why don't you give me your raincoat. Can I get you something to drink?'

His father shook his head. Then he stretched full length and took a deep breath, smiling all the while.

'No, this is fine,' he said. 'It's about to rain, I can feel it. Beautiful spot you've got here. Is it like this in the daytime too?'

'Better. Especially for Marisa and the baby.'

'Marisa and the baby. You must have a lot to tell me, eh?'

The young man felt his jaw go slack. In his dreams, his father always knew the latest about everything that had happened to the family.

'Yes, I suppose I do.'

'Naturally I'm not expecting you to fill me in on current events. Let's skip politics, work, the world at large, if possible. Domestic matters, that's what I care about. Your sisters, you, Marisa, the baby. Those things.'

He was surprised that his father used the word 'domestic'. And even more that he would have mentioned everyone except Mother, but the son did not know what to say.

'I'm going to help myself to some whisky. Sure you won't have any?'

'No, thanks. By the way, lights in the swimming pool – that's some idea.'

'It's not mine,' the son said, going inside. 'The house, I mean.' Coming back with a full glass, he realized that they had not yet touched. He stopped behind his father's chair. 'I thought you could see everything that was going on here from where you were.'

His father gazed round him, slowly, one way and then the other. 'Sadly not. It's not like people imagine.'

The son looked at the swimming pool and sensed he was not in control of what he was saying nor of what he was about to say.

'You'd be amazed by all the things I did for you these last few years, thinking that you were looking at me.' And he laughed a bit, joylessly but without resentment, as if to empty his lungs. 'So you know nothing about these past four years? Incredible.'

The father shifted in the deck chair and gave his son a sidelong glance.

'There may be changes where they're sending us now. If it's of any consolation to you.'

The son stared at him, puzzled.

'There's been a transfer. From now on, I'll be somewhere else. Not only me, many others too. Things are not as organized there as people think. Sometimes the unexpected happens. Like my being here with you now.'

'But why me? Why haven't you gone to see Mum?'

For a moment or two, the father looked at the wavy light of the pool. A slight change came over his face, a faint trace of sadness.

'It would have been harder with your mother. One night isn't much, and I need you to tell me all you can. Your mother and I would have talked about other matters. Mostly about the past – ourselves, the good times we had together. And that would have been unfair of me.' He paused. 'There are things that are technically impossible in my present state – feeling, for example. Do you follow me? To a certain extent, what I am tonight is something your mother wouldn't much appreciate. With you it's a lot simpler. Your memory is quite . . . selective, let us say; you always took an objective view of emotions. Towards your mother, towards your sisters, towards yourself. So be it.' He paused again. 'I also thought you'd be better able to cope with the feelings this visit of mine would arouse in you. When it comes down to it, I was never all that important to you, was I?'

An emotion came over the son that he had not had for a long time – a kind of submissiveness and a need to fight against it. He knew at once that in the last four years he had not been what he was again now – his father's son. He went to the edge of the pool, took off his loafers, and sat down with his legs in the water.

'If you hadn't been so important, I would never have done the things I did for you these last years. Didn't that ever occur to you?'

'No.'

The terse reply left the son bewildered. It was so brutal that it sounded sincere – and for that very reason unlikely. Cowardly. Almost unfair.

'And now you know – what?' he said straight out.

'Nothing,' his father answered. Then he stood up, dragged the deck chair to the edge of the pool, and sat with his hands in his pockets. 'I suppose nothing changes. What you did, you did. It's pointless getting angry about that now – with yourself or with me. Isn't it?'

Not only was it pointless but, in view of his father's state, the son began to feel that it was not his place to question anything or to behave with such uncharacteristic belligerence. The need to stand up to his father vanished, and only the submissiveness remained, no longer directed at him but at a state of affairs, at an obtuse, intangible abstraction.

'You're right,' he said. 'I'm sorry.'

For a moment or two, neither of them spoke.

'Anyway, I was exaggerating a bit,' the son then said. 'There weren't all that many things I did thinking of you.'

The father let out a little laugh. 'So I thought.'

In the distance, a flash of lightning cut the sky in two. When the thunder came the father shrugged, and again the son heard the little laugh.

'I had almost forgotten such things. It's interesting how memory works, what it retains and what it drops.'

'The crickets,' the son said. 'Do you hear them? They were keeping me awake. That's how I happened to be up when you arrived.' He hesitated. The crickets? He thought better of it and decided to say no more.

'All right,' said the father in a very low voice. 'Let's get down to what we have to.'

'First, may I ask you something?'

The deck chair creaked. The son strained to keep his eyes on his father.

'As you like. But you know how it is. Once you learn

[49]

something, it's hard to erase it from your mind. No threat intended. I just want you to know.'

'I understand,' the son said. Then, his voice hesitant, he asked, 'Does everyone go to the same place? Doesn't it matter what each person has done?'

'I could have answered that when I was twenty years old. I always suspected that what one did mattered more in life than afterwards. As for your other question, where we go is not exactly a place. But yes, since we are all relatively equal everyone goes there. Your way of life and your neighbour's are as different, for example, as your height from his. A nuance – and nuances don't count. Basically there are two states, yours and mine. It's a lot more complicated, but you wouldn't understand now.'

'So you and I are going to meet again at some point,' the son said.

His father did not answer.

'Is it of any importance to be together there?'

His father did not answer.

'What's it like?' the son said.

His father averted his eyes and looked at the pool.

'Like swimming in the dark,' he said. The wavy light gleamed on his face. 'Like swimming in the dark in an immense pool without ever growing tired.'

The son downed the rest of his whisky in a single gulp and waited for it to reach his stomach. Then he threw the ice into the pool and put the empty glass down.

'What else do you want to know?' asked his father.

The son shook his head. He moved his legs a little in the water and looked at the base of the deck chair, at the raincoat, and at his father's relaxed, mildly timeless face. He thought about how reticent they had always been in all physical contact and how the hugs and kisses his father had given him in his dreams now seemed unbelievably naïve and false. This was reality: everything going on just as before, both of them picking up almost from the point where they had broken off nearly four years earlier. Even if only for one night.

'Where shall I start?' the son said.

'Wherever you like. Don't worry about time. We have all night. The sun won't come up until you finish.'

The son took a deep breath and let it out slowly, knowing that he had entered the longest, most secret night of his life. He began, of course, with his daughter.

ANOTHER KIND OF CINDERELLA

Angela Huth

'Now come along, gentlemen, *if* you please,' urged Lewis Crone, waving his baton. 'What we want is a little more *up*lift in the last bar, don't we? Up, up and *away*...'

'Stuff it, Lew,' murmured Reginald Breen, second violinist, under his breath.

He dabbed at the sweat on his forehead with a large white handkerchief. It was bloody hot down here in the pit, even in winter. And he was damned if he'd give the last bar a lift. It wasn't exactly Beethoven the Winterstown Concert Orchestra were struggling to bring some life to, after all. Just wallpaper music to fill the gap where the Fairy blooming Godmother turned the mice into ponies. They hadn't half had some trouble with the ponies this year, what's more – doing their business just at the wrong moment, and so on. Reginald sniffed.

'So once again, gentlemen,' the mighty Lewis, conductor with airs above his station, was saying. 'We'll take it once again, *if* you please.'

What's the point, Reginald wondered, in being this particular for this kind of show? Not a soul in the audience would notice whether or not there was a wretched uplift in the last bar. Half of them would be under twelve. The other half, pensioners' outings, were plugged into hearing aids. For them a pantomime was no different from a silent film. He tucked his instrument under his chin, turned with an exaggerated look of scorn to his friend, Tom, first violin.

'Better give it the works,' whispered Tom, 'or he'll keep us into the dinner hour.'

'Righty-ho. Last time. Up, up and *away*.' Reginald had perfected his mimicry over the years.

He and Tom lifted their bows in unison. Tom caught the conductor's agitated eye. The orchestra crashed once more into the last few lines of forgettable music. Their sudden energy came from indignation. Lewis Crone had kept them at it since ten this morning. They were now hungry, bored and fed up with his absurd attention to detail. Trouble was, Lewis had once seen André Previn rehearsing an orchestra on television. Since then he had applied his own version of Previn's methods to the WCO, causing much suffering and discontent. In the old days they'd played through the score a couple of times at the beginning of the season – *Jack and the Beanstalk, Aladdin, Mother Goose,* whatever – and that was it. Now, all this per-nickety fussing was driving them to near rebellion. Most of the players – weary professional men – had considered resigning, but none actually did so. There were not many openings for their class of musicians on the south coast. Tom was the most vociferous in his complaints. Reginald encouraged him in his discontent, for Tom's resignation would be to Reginald's own benefit. Once Tom had gone he, Reginald, would surely become first violin. He had waited some thirty years for this position. Over and over again others, outrageously, had been placed above him – incompetent musicians, mostly, from out-side the orchestra. And once, worst of all, a very junior 'tal-ented' violinist from the WCO itself. He hadn't lasted long: no stamina. Many times Reginald had suffered the humiliation of being passed over, and had kept his silence and his hope. He could not afford to resign.

The morning's rehearsal over, Tom and Reginald made their way along the front. They exchanged few words: music was their only common interest. Proper music. Tom carried his violin case under his arm. Home, this afternoon, Tom would be practising the Mozart concerto. Reginald would be attending to his mother.

The sea breeze on their faces was good after the stuffiness of the orchestra pit. Reginald always enjoyed the short walk home. It refreshed him, gave him strength for the tasks ahead.

'Still haven't got the coach finished, I hear,' said Tom.

'Coach and beanstalk, it's the same every year, always late.' Reginald smiled at the thought of the familiar incompetence.

'At least we'll see Valerie in her spangles, tomorrow.' Tom was something of a woman's man, keenly sensitive to the potential of leading ladies.

'She's as good a Cinderella as I can remember, I'll say that.' Reginald himself had been quite taken with her – what he could see from the pit – during the past month of rehearsals.

As the men parted, Tom paused for a last look out to sea. There was a fishing boat on the horizon.

'Give anything to be out there,' he muttered, more to himself than to his friend. 'Always fancied playing on the deck of a boat, up and down in time with the waves.' He gave a small, helpless laugh. Reginald smiled in reply. He, too, had known fantasies that would never materialize.

He slowed his pace, once Tom had gone. He was always reluctant to return home and face *that* kind of music : but face it he must, as he told himself every day. If he didn't hurry and buy his mother her paper there would be more to answer for.

'Is that you, Reginald?'

The familiar peevish tone bit into his ears as soon as he was through the door. Who the hell do you think it is, he wanted to shout back. Who else would let themselves in at 12.55 precisely, as he did five days a week?

'It's me, Mother, all right,' he called, and clenched his fists, taking a grip on himself before going into the front room.

Mrs Breen sat in an armchair in the bow window. Her vastly swollen legs hung from widely parted knees, slippered feet not quite touching the floor. A mustard crochet cardigan – made in the days when she still bothered to sew the crochet squares together – covered a bosom so cumbersome she was unable to see her own hands in its shade. But the fingers (the worst kind of sausages, Reginald thought, among other savage thoughts) worked skilfully on their own, crocheting away, square after square, hour after hour. The furious, pale eyes, scowling on their ledge of fat purple cheek, were attending to some cooking programme on the television. Mrs Breen had not moved since Reginald had left her that morning. She was not able to move on her own. Her illness meant she was almost completely immobile, though Reginald had reason to think that on secret occasions, when she wanted something badly enough, she was able to reach it. Chocolates in the tin on the bookshelf, for instance. Their unaccountable disappearance, observed by Reginald on many occasions when his mother was in bed, could only mean one thing. But the time had not yet come to challenge her.

Her mauvish bulk backlit by the netted light from the window, Mrs Breen made no effort to drag her eyes from the television.

'I fancy the Ambrosia today, Reginald,' she said, 'with that tin of plums you got last Friday.'

Incapable of shopping herself, her recall of exactly what her son had bought, when, was extraordinary. She would plan the life of half a pound of cheddar down to the last slice, insistent that only an ounce should be used for the sauce for the macaroni, and the merest scrapings for the Tuesday cheese supper with biscuits and tomatoes. Should Reginald miscalculate, and the cheese be finished before its allotted time, Mrs Breen would be moved to one of her famous rages when every blood vessel in her body enlarged, darkened, and threatened to burst through her glowering skin.

'Anything else?'

'Tin of curried spaghetti still there, is it?'

'It is.'

Reginald's heart pounded in relief. Last night he had had half a mind to eat it, but had resisted on the ground that he had had no energy to ask his mother's permission.

'Then I'll have that.'

Reginald went to the kitchen to set about opening tins and preparing the tray. The room faced north. Any light that managed to challenge the old curtain at the window was diffused by the coarse-grained and very dirty net. A smell of disinfectant clashed with smells of years of frugal meals. Opening the window was forbidden, so the air was never cleared. The kitchen gave Reginald a headache every day. He dreaded it. But there was no escape. How many years, now? Eight? Almost nine. And how many more . . . ?

When he had placed his mother's tray of lunch beside her, he returned to the kitchen. But he could not face either washing up last night's supper dishes and the breakfast, or making himself a sandwich. Instead, he went out to the strip of ill-kept grass that was the back garden. When his father had been alive, herbaceous borders ran down both sides – borders that kept the old man's every spare moment fully occupied. From the thin earth he had managed to persuade a magnificent show of hollyhocks, tulips, dahlias (his speciality) – the lot. But Reginald could never be bothered with gardening. Everything had gone to seed, died off years ago. Now the lawn was bordered with weeds. But the apple tree, the single tree in the Breen family possession, still blossomed. And the blackbird still lived there. Reginald listened to its song now – vibrant, optimistic notes that gave him the courage to go on, sometimes. He lit a cigarette. Into his mind came a picture of Valerie, who in tomorrow's dress rehearsal would be in all her finery at the ball. He looked forward to that. He found himself pecking quite fast at the cigarette, then grinding its stub under his heel with a force that surprised him. Valerie was the sort of girl, had things been different, Reginald might well have approached. He had no great ambitions concerning her, of course, even in his imagination. With the difference in their ages, marriage was naturally out of the question. No: all he wanted, or told himself he wanted, was a friend. Her funny crooked smile and short bouncy hair inspired him with exciting ideas of friendship. Perhaps one day he would summon the courage to speak to her, see how things went.

'Reg! It's time.'

Reginald allowed himself a moment's more reflection, and returned to his mother. It was time for the dreaded visit to the bathroom, the ungainly negotiating of the dim passage, the old woman's entire weight on his arm, her invective spewing in his ear. Then, the long afternoon. He would have liked to go to his room, have another go at the Tchaikovsky. But his mother could hear, she said, however quietly he played. It hurt her ears, all that screeching, she said – she had always wanted Reginald to go into insurance, like his father. The violin was forbidden in the house.

Instead of music, it would be shopping at the Co-op, hoovering the stairs, two hours of bad-tempered Scrabble, another tray for high tea, television, and the terrible ritual of putting Mrs Breen to bed. By the time Reginald went to his own room he was exhausted. Like a disobedient child, he would play his radio under the bedclothes for a while, very loud. This was the part of the day he most looked forward to. Much though he enjoyed his nightly blast of illicit music, it put him to sleep almost at once.

On the notice-board at the stage door it was announced that the transformation scene was the first to be rehearsed. Reginald felt a slight pricking of anticipation as he undid his violin case, took out the instrument and wiped its bow. The awkward notes of his fellow musicians, tuning up, usually filled him with gloom and unease as he faced the long morning of indifferent music ahead. Today the squawks of striving notes could not touch him. He tried out a few notes himself, tightened a couple of strings. He scarcely noticed Lewis Crone blundering up on the podium, cocky, grinning, one hand fingering a yellow tie.

'Making a statement, what?' whispered Tom, who was polishing his violin with a duster – a very superior instrument which could not have been better cared for had it been a Stradivarius.

'Won't get anywhere,' replied Reginald. He had no idea why he made this comment, or if there was any truth in his speculation.

The stage lights were switched on, bringing life to the Ugly Sisters' grim kitchen.

'Idiot,' yelled a voice from off-stage. 'That's the ballroom effing light.'

The peach light was dimmed, replaced by the kind of light usually glowing in the front room at Reginald's house. No wonder Cinderella, shortly to be sitting by the giant fireplace, needed a Fairy Godmother. Reginald could have done with one most days himself.

Bev Birley, in fishnet tights and a short satin tunic, came striding on to the stage. Bev was Prince Charming. Last year she had been Jack, the year before Aladdin. Beginning to show her years, too, thought Reginald, noting the definite thickness of her hips. He had never liked Bev – not that he had ever had occasion to talk to her. But she was stuck-up, haughty, tongue like a whiplash to junior members of the cast, though all agreeable smiles to visiting stars. Between seasons, Reginald saw her sometimes in the town walking a terrier. Once, he recognized her picture in the window of an optician. She was wearing flyaway blue-tinted glasses and her hair had been stuck down with grease. She still did not look very nice. Presumably, not being in national demand, she had to do any job she could to keep herself going between seasons.

'Anyone wanting me this morning?' Bev shouted into the darkness of the auditorium, legs spread wide, hands on hips, her annual stance in every proposal scene. There was a slight titter in the orchestra pit. Tom nodded towards Lewis. Bev scowled.

'No one wanting you till two, darling,' the director called from the back of the stalls. 'See you then.'

Bev stomped off.

'Stuck-up bit, know what I'd like to do to her,' whispered Tom.

Reginald had no time to imagine what this might be because Cinderella came on to the stage just then, wrapped in a large cloak. She wore a great deal of scarlet lipstick which made her crooked smile look very grown up. As Bev passed her, she whispered something that made them both smile, and ruffled her hair.

'Cheek,' said Tom.

'Taking liberties, sucking up, usual thing,' agreed Reginald.

'Quiet now.' Paddy Ever, the director – or Ever Anxious, as he was known – had moved forward to take command. He leaned over the pit and shouted up at the stage.

'Why are we wearing a cloak, darling, in the kitchen?' Cinderella, Reginald could see, looked confused.

'Wardrobe said it was a cloak for this scene. Suppose I'm cold in this bloody great kitchen, no central heating.'

The musicians smiled among themselves. At the beginning of the day they were ready to respond to any kind of joke, no matter how feeble.

Paddy scratched his head. 'I mean, *would* Cinderella suddenly be in a cloak? *Why* would she be in a cloak, now, but only in a dress in the last scene? Is it viable, is all I'm asking. Is it *rational*?'

Paddy's worries were known to hold up proceedings, sometimes for ages. The musicians flicked their music, rested their instruments. They could be in for a long spell of problem-thrashing before Lewis requested their first chord.

'Don't be daft, Pad: cloak on, amazing quick change in the dark. Stands to reason.'

Paddy's face briefly relaxed. Reginald did not envy him his job. 'Ball dress under ... point taken, darling. But why the sudden lipstick?'

They could hear Cinderella sigh. 'Can't put lipstick on in the dark, can I?'

'Righty-ho, lipstick on. Let's go.'

The Winterstown pantomime was all a very different kettle of fish to the Palladium, Reginald thought, as he did every year.

The rehearsal began. Cinderella and the Fairy Godmother, a dear old thing who had been in panto for years and whose underarms, these days, swung as the wand waved, played the scene too far downstage for Reginald to see anything. He could only just hear Valerie's sweet voice and strange emphasis. 'Oh, god*mother* ...' He liked such original rendering.

It wasn't till after the mid-morning coffee break the musicians were required to play the few high notes whose purpose, as Lewis so often explained, was to convey excitement. There was drama with the ponies, as usual: two nasty little Shetlands, hired at great expense from an animal psychiatrist, but who had minds of their own just the same. They refused to stand still, and laid back their ears warning what would happen should they be pressed to act against their will. One of them nipped young Andrew, the coachman. A part-time actor mostly out of work, Andrew proudly admitted he started off at the bottom year after year, but remained convinced that one day his moment would come. Trouble was, as he once confided to Reg, he was so nervous of the ponies, despite their small size, that it was all he could do to keep holding their reins, let alone think himself deeply into the part of the coachman. A lamp fell off the coach soon after Andrew returned from being bandaged, and then the door wouldn't open. 'Bloody useless wand,' snapped the old godmother, longing for her lunchtime Guinness, as the carpenter hammered away at the door.

It was a morning full of laughs – the kind of morning that made up for so much of the aching boredom of the job. And at last Cinderella appeared alone in the spotlight, cloakless, dazzling in a dress of sequins splattered on to net. Reginald still could not see her properly: he would have to wait for her upstage number, 'I'm going to the ball', for that. As it was, the wolf whistles and laughs from the stagehands – an old tradition at any leading lady's first dress rehearsal – made him uncomfortable. For all its good humour, Reginald did not like the idea of Valerie in all her finery being laughed at.

At the lunch break, Reginald hurried out alone from the pit. He had to break the news to his mother – whose dinner was, thank God, provided by Meals on Wheels today – that there was to be an unscheduled rehearsal this afternoon, due to delays this morning caused by the coach and ponies. Her outrage was predictable. He would have to listen to ten minutes of abuse and insult – 'If you were Sir Thomas blinking Beecham I might understand' – before providing her with a calming glass of brandy and making his escape. Dreading the scene ahead, he barged clumsily round the corner that led to the stage door, and bumped into Valerie herself. She was still in her ball dress. The sequins, in the poor winter light, looked asleep.

'Excuse me, I'm so sorry . . .'

'Reg, isn't it?' Cinderella gave him a wonderful smile. Her grasp of every name in the company endeared her to all.

'I have to let my mother know . . .'

'Like the dress? Isn't it gross?' She laughed. 'See you later.'

Reginald spun home, weightless. His mother's fury, the cold sausage for his lunch, the smell of the kitchen, the jibes at his general uselessness, meant nothing to him. Impervious to everything but the extraordinary thumping of his heart, inspired by Cinderella's smile, he was in and out of the house with astonishing speed. As he hurried back up the garden path, almost enjoying his mother's wailing in his ears, Reginald knew he was in love with Cinderella, and was to spend the afternoon playing for her alone while she danced above him at the ball.

In the next two weeks of rehearsal, Reginald did not run into Valerie backstage again. But in his new state of love he was quite happy to be patient, to hear her sweet voice above him, hear the tapping of her feet, and to catch the occasional glimpse of her when she was upstage. Her prancing little body and enchanting smile were particularly appealing in her ragged dress, though he saw her best at the ball: the choreographer had naturally arranged for the prince to waltz with his Cinderella as far upstage as possible. Reginald, putting his soul into every note of the banal waltz, followed her steps as Bev swung her about. They gazed into each other's eyes, the woman and the girl, acting the kind of happiness which was so convincing it caused Reginald a jealous stab. Fact was, they were much better actors than he had ever given them credit for. The audience would believe this was Prince Charming – not Bev the part-time optician's model – in love with Cinderella, not Valerie who, Reginald knew, sometimes sang in a pub to make ends meet.

He longed for an event that he knew would never happen: waltzing *himself* with Cinderella in some posh hotel ballroom with chandeliers, far from Winterstown. Then on the balcony of their suite, the moonlight and roses bit: he would play a little tune – one of his own compositions, maybe, while she sipped champagne. Next, he would kiss her, so hard she could no longer smile. After that . . . but there his fantasies stalled. He could only imagine a paling dawn sky.

None of that would ever happen. It was some consolation, watching her, to know that at least *this* was all make-believe. What Reginald could not have borne would have been Val (she had become Val in his mind) dancing, in real life, with another man. He closed his eyes as he pulled the final note from his violin. He longed.

At the first performance of *Cinderella*, as always, there was a full house. The audience, mostly pensioners and schoolchildren, loved it. Val, taking many bows, had never looked so appealing. She and Prince Charming held hands and smiled copiously at each other. Reginald would have liked to have gone round to her dressing-room and joined the crowd of admirers he presumed would be there, tell her she was wonderful. As it was, he had to hurry. His mother would be furious at his lateness caused by the prolonged applause.

Once again, he ran into Valerie, surprisingly, in the passage that led to the dressing-rooms. She was still in her ball dress, an old cardigan slung around her shoulders.

'Good first house, wasn't it?'

Reginald nodded. The compliments rose, then withered, in his throat.

'Bev and I are just off for a hamburger. See you.'

She was gone.

On his way home, Reginald decided what to do – for now, he believed, he should waste no more time, act fast. He would send her flowers. Huge great bunch in cellophane, small card in the envelope saying *From a secret admirer*. The thought of this plan went some way to dispelling his fury with himself for not speaking to her. She must think him a useless old man. But time would change all that. Plans beginning to crowd his head, he opened the front door.

'Is that you, Reg?' His mother's shriek was more than usually annoyed.

Protected from her by his inner strategies, Reginald went calmly to deal with her cocoa, the wearying process of putting her to bed, and all the arrows of her fury.

Reginald dreamed that night of himself and Cinderella at a princely ball, but he never sent the flowers. He managed to leave early enough, next morning, to get to the florist before rehearsals for a concert. But he was so confused by the scents and colours and prices, he left without buying. He'd had in mind pure white lilies, or cream old-fashioned roses mixed with cornflowers – the kind of thing his father had been so proud of in his border. The florist seemed to have only crude red or rust flowers on stiff stems, leaves unbending as swords. Nothing worthy of Cinderella.

Then, just as he was coming out of the shop – the assistant's eyes contemptuous on his back – he observed Val and Bev walking down the other side of the High Street. Both wore jeans and anoraks. For a moment it was quite hard to recognize them. They paused, kissed each other on the cheek, and Bev disappeared into Boots. Valerie, turning to continue on her way, saw Reginald. She waved, smiled her glorious smile, arming him for the day against all adversities.

There were plenty of those. At the rehearsal for a concert in the Winterstown Hall, Lewis was at his most waspish and petulant, quibbling with Tom's tone and Reg's high C, and sneering so hard at poor old Jim Reed on the drums it was a wonder the man did not resign on the spot. But as his bow soared through the Enigma Variations, transporting him to the English countryside in May, walking in meadowlands with Cinderella, it came to Reg that the only way to make any progress with Val was to do something. Like ask her out for a drink.

At the lunch break that day the other members of the orchestra left for an hour in the pub. Reginald could not be persuaded to join them. He wanted to be on his own: Meals on Wheels was dealing with his mother. There was no reason to move.

He sat, violin across his knees, in the forest of empty chairs on the stage. The music played on in his ears, not disturbing the real silence. Down in the vast hall, chairs were stacked against the walls ready to be regimented for the next concert. A thin rain pattered against high windows. The light on the bare walls was dull as old stone, and it was cold. But Reginald spent an undisturbed lunch hour, oblivious of everything around him, walking with Valerie in Herefordshire (a place he had always longed to visit). He was, for once, at peace.

After the performance that night he hurried to the stage door, and then out into the alleyway at the back of the theatre. It was still raining, a cold hard rain that damply spotted his mackintosh. He stood, eyes on the square light of the glass door, violin case under one arm, heart pumping audibly. Members of the cast and orchestra came out in groups, and singly. Once a show was under way, nobody planned much of a social life after performances. They were all keen to get home.

Almost last, Valerie emerged. She wore a scarf wound high round her neck, but no hat. In the rain, and from the light within, the frizzy mop of her hair glittered like a swarm of fireflies. Behind her, Bev was talking to the porter at the stage door. She wore an imitation leopardskin coat and seemed to be cross about something. Val saw Reg.

'What's up, darling?' she asked.

Reg moved his free hand on to the solid, familiar curves of his violin case.

'I was wondering', he said, 'if you'd care for a quick drink on your way home?'

He deliberately said quick because there was not much time. He had taken the precaution of making up some story to his mother about having to see the manager, but her credulity would not stretch far. Half an hour's grace, at the most.

Val laughed. It was not a friendly laugh. But perhaps sound was distorted here, out in the rain.

'Why not?' she said. 'Bev and I and some of the others are going down to the Drake. Want to join us?'

Reg paused for a second. Val's idea did not fit in with his plan at all. The last thing he wanted was to be with her in a crowd, perhaps unable to exchange a word. He wanted her to himself, just a small table, somewhere, between them. He wanted her full attention while he told her some of the things that had been piling within him for as long as he could remember, and had never been spoken. His violin had been the sole recipient of his feelings, the music his only consolation. But man cannot live by music alone as Tom, who had many an eager woman on his arm, so often said.

'I don't think I will, thanks. My mother . . .'

'Very well. Another time.' Val was not interested. But then, something of the approaching Christmas spirit, Reginald supposed it was, entered her funny little head. She decided to be kind. 'But tell you what: tomorrow after the matinée? Bev's going to the dentist so we can't go over to her mum as per usual. We could have a coffee.'

'A coffee?'

A kaleidoscope of difficulties swooped through Reg's brain. More excuses to his mother would have to be thought up, and where would be a suitable place to go?

'Very well,' he said.

'Meet you here after the show, then. Bev!'

Bev hurried out, glanced at Reg. Val was all smiles.

'Blimey, what a night.' Bev snapped up an umbrella, put her arm round Val, drawing her beneath it. 'Cheers, Reg,' Bev said, and Reginald watched Val slip her arm into the crook of nylon leopardskin.

They moved away, in step, huddled snugly under the umbrella, confident of its shelter, like those people in the advertisement for a life insurance company. Reginald waited till they were out of sight. Then, hugging his violin case, he turned into the full blast of the rain in the direction of home.

Reginald and Val sat at a small table in the window of the Wimpy Bar – nearest eating place to the theatre. Reginald had suggested they go to the tearooms further down the High Street, altogether a more comfortable place, but Val had insisted she fancied chips in the Wimpy.

Two cups of thin coffee sat between them. Val covered her chips with spurts of ketchup from a plastic tomato. Reginald kept one hand on his violin case, propped up beside him. His head was empty from lack of sleep. He was drained, exhausted, by his imaginings. He didn't know where to begin. Ten minutes of their half-hour had passed, and all he had done was to make a disparaging remark about Lewis Crone. Val had disagreed. She said far as she was concerned he was a good sport.

'It must be boring down in the pit,' she said eventually, 'not seeing anything.'

'You can see enough. I get a good view of you dancing in the ball scene.'

'That!' Val laughed, more friendly than last night. 'See Bev treading on my toes? She's a horrible dancer.'

She laid one hand flat on the formica table-top, examined her nails with great interest as she slightly lifted each finger in turn. Reginald wanted to cover her hand with his.

'You're a lovely dancer, though,' he said.

[70]

Val gave him a teasing look. 'Reg! Haven't you got a wife, a woman? Someone? You always look so down in the dumps.'

'There's my mother to be looked after.' Reg suppressed a sigh and tapped his violin case. 'There's my music. I'm all right, just not one of life's jokers.'

'No.'

The speech Reg had rehearsed most of the night, inspired by Bach under the bedclothes, welled. It was now or never, he thought.

'But I'd like to get to know you – nothing . . . out of line. Cup of tea sometimes. Talk. You know. I haven't much of a life socially. What with my mother. Drink with Tom, Saturdays. End of a concert drink with the boys. Not occasions to talk . . .'

Reg petered out, aware he had lost the thread of his message. The rubbish he was talking sounded close to self-pity. He didn't want Val's pity: last thing he wanted. And she had stopped picking at her chips. She pushed her empty cup away, stiff-handed. Gave a tight little smile, as if she decided she must get through this little scene as graciously as possible, but it was boring.

'Poor old Reg. Well, it's fine by me if we have another coffee some time. Though I'm leaving Winterstown, March. Doing three months in Manchester, an Agatha Christie.'

Reginald's heart contracted. He would have to think about that later: the bleakness of the spring.

'Anyway,' she smiled, nicely this time, 'you must be ten years older than me, Reg.'

'Probably.'

It was dark outside now. The pair of them made awkward shapes reflected in the plate glass window. Madness seized Reg so fast he was unable to control it, to reason with himself.

'But I'm over the moon about you, see. Nothing bothersome, mind. Just, watching you dancing away, Cinderella in her ballgown, I fancied your pretty smile was for me. Daft, I know.' He saw her look of alarm, tried to slow himself. 'All I want is to talk to you, don't I? To tell you things, give you a good time, spend my savings on you. I've a fair bit put on one side – nothing to spend my wages on all these years. What do you think, Val? Would you let me, sometimes?'

Val gave a small laugh, perturbed. 'I don't want anything like that, nice though you are.'

'No. Well. I didn't rate my chances high.'

'It's not that I'd mind a chat from time to time. But Bev wouldn't like it. There'd be trouble. I've had enough trouble.'

'Trouble with Bev?'

'Bev's my friend.'

'I know Bev's your friend. But she can't order your life about. A woman.'

Val sighed. 'Have to be going,' she said. 'Meeting her at six.'

'Meeting Bev? What's she got, this Bev?'

In his confusion, Reg could not be sure of anything. But for a moment – so short he might have imagined it – he thought Val looked scared.

'A nasty temper if things don't go her way.'

'You shouldn't put up with her. I mean, do you *like* her?' Later, Reg reflected, his boldness may have been impertinent.

Val shrugged. 'Thanks for the coffee 'n' chips.' She stood up, swirling the scarf round her neck.

'Cinderella,' said Reg. 'Cinderella.'

She bent briefly towards him. He could smell her breath: ketchup, chips, coffee. She patted his shoulder.

'Chin up, Reg.'

'I want you to know' – her hand fled from his shoulder – 'that every performance it's you I'm playing for, Val, down there, all that rubbishy music. One day I could play you Brahms, on a beach somewhere, tide coming in, never go back to the orchestra. They'll never make me first violin is what I'm afraid of, not even when Tom goes. You could, you could come with –'

Val turned from his jibbering, impatient. Reg could tell from her eyes she thought he was a silly old fool, letting go.

'What you must remember is this, Reg.' Her voice was harsh as flint now, cutting the quick of him. 'You're a nice guy, but I'm another kind of Cinderella.'

She was gone. Striding through the purplish light, the ketchup tables, the bleak landscape of formica and burgers. Reginald remained standing, clutching his violin case, peering through the window. In the late-night shopping crowds he thought he glimpsed a leopardskin coat, but of Val he could see nothing.

That night he kept his eyes on the music, did not look up to see Cinderella in her ball dress dancing with Bev the prince. Reg had always known she was not for him, any more than was the position of first violin. But who was she for? What did she mean, another kind of Cinderella?

After the performance he hurried off to avoid an accidental meeting. It was a night full of ironic stars. Just twenty-four hours ago, in the rain, she had given him some hope. He didn't know why he bothered with hope, any more.

'Is that you, Reg?' Furious voice. Usual thing.

Reg made his way slowly across the small, stuffy hall and into the front room. He opened the door, surveyed the familiar picture of the monstrous old woman who was his mother: the mother who had messed up his entire life. Plumped up with indignation, she sat upright in her chair, accusation flaring across her purple cheeks, obscene legs swinging. If it hadn't been for his binding duty to her, things would have been different. If he had been a worse son, he would have had a better chance.

'What kept you then? Dancing with Cinderella?'

She gave a sneering laugh, thumping one swollen hand into the soft mess of crochet on her knee. Reginald swung his violin case above his head, and moved towards her in silence before they both screamed.

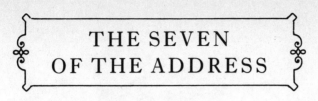

THE SEVEN
OF THE ADDRESS

Chaim Potok

Ilana Davita Chandal had lost her way. Over the past two decades, her baroque style, with its stinging wit, soaring rhythms, arabesque whorls, and Latinate prose, had earned her critical praise, prestigious awards, honorary degrees, and a cultlike following. Known simply as 'I. D.' to her devoted readers, whose paucity in numbers was more than offset by their élitist erudition and academic pre-eminence, she had come recently to a crossroads in her work, and then had halted, feeling witless, wrung dry.

Deep into middle age, her hair gray, her eyes frequently achy and fluttery behind thick shell-rimmed glasses, her heart thudding mysteriously at odd moments of the day or night, she had begun to sense piercingly the chill touch of The End. Her subject was the modern intellectual poised amid the relativities of secularism yet sensing from time to time the obtrusive beckonings of the world of tradition. She admitted to herself the possibility that she may have plumbed that subject to its depths, drained it of its fructifying waters, and was now stuck knee-deep in its muddy bottom.

And so she put away her pen – an ancient black Waterman with a pliant nib and the original rubber bladder, a gift in her teens from her encouraging mother; I. D. wrote her early drafts in longhand and had the callus on her right middle finger to prove it – and busied herself with matters having to do with The Community. She typed letters to the Op-Ed page of the *New York Times* about feminist issues and the Arab uprising in Israel. She appeared in forums sponsored by PEN. She attended literary receptions in elegant New York hotels. At university gatherings, she gave erudite talks on Virginia Woolf, Henry James, and the role of the artist in post-modern culture, 'a culture so insipid and attenuated,' as she put it, 'that it doesn't even have its own name.'

One week in April, her fifth month in Muddy Bottom – she had by then given that name to this time and place in her life – she accepted an invitation to attend a conference during the coming June in Jerusalem and deliver a paper in English on a recently deceased modern Israeli writer of world stature. 'Change place, change luck,' she remembered her mother once saying.

I. D. knew little modern Hebrew. Unfamiliar with this writer's work, she began to read him in English translation. Each work she read added to her astonishment. His range, wit, and imagination were remarkably contemporary; yet his locutions, his words and rhythms, echoed with archaisms from a literature long gone. Word-games, allusions, ambiguity, lengthy passages of dreamlike free-association, the family as a battleground, man lost in a hostile or indifferent world – these were his subjects, recounted in sentences resonant with the rhetoric and rhythms of holy rabbis and medieval bards. The voice was the voice of the modernist, yet the hands were the hands of the past.

Over a salad niçoise lunch at Au Grenier near Columbia University, a fellow American writer knowledgeable in Hebrew pointed out to her phrases in the great man's prose that yielded many levels of meaning simultaneously because the language was layered with millennia of nuances. She listened, gazed at her barely touched tuna, and berated herself: How had she missed that author during all the years she had grown up reading Henry James, Virginia Woolf, James Joyce, T. S.

Eliot? Why had she accepted the invitation to the conference? How would she ever write and deliver a paper on an author she could barely read in the original before an erudite academic audience gathered at a university in that author's home town? She would need to find that writer's Right Address: his core, his nucleus, his essence. She had labored years before discovering the Right Address of Henry James. And Virginia Woolf – she did not want to think again of the effort she had put into ferreting out *that* Address!

'So what's I. D. doing these days?' the knowledgeable writer asked amiably, eager for her response.

She mumbled something about her mother's illness keeping her from work the past few months, and felt lost in a landscape of deepest darkness.

Her husband said to her that evening, 'People who don't eat tend to die. It's a known fact.' He was an intense, bearded, balding man who taught philosophy at Columbia and mysticism at the Jewish Theological Seminary.

'I can't get into him,' she mumbled. 'The style, the structure. He eludes me.'

'Three weeks you're reading him, you already want to get into him?'

'Time is short.'

'Listen, addresses no one finds overnight. How long did it take with James? And Eliot, that anti-Semite? How long before you got into Eliot?'

'I was an idiot to accept the invitation.'

'Eat. Dead from anorexia you won't see him. That you can be sure about. The dead don't visit the dead.'

During the next four weeks, she continued to read with feverish passion the books of the deceased writer. One night she dreamed terribly of Faulkner's Popeye standing on the scaffold and asking the sheriff to smooth back his hair. 'Fix my hair, Jack,' she distinctly heard him say. 'Sure, I'll fix it for you,' the sheriff said; and sprang the trap. She woke sweating, her heart thundering in her ears.

Haggard, forlorn, her paper still unwritten, I. D. flew to Israel.

She arrived at Ben Gurion Airport after a sleepless night aboard a jetliner jammed with Gospel-singing pilgrims from Des Moines, noisy teenagers from Long Island, and restless Hasidim from Brooklyn. She walked in a daze through passport control, found her valise, rolled her cart through the customs green line, and stepped into a tumultuous mass of jostling taxi drivers, dark-garbed and bearded Hasidim, muscular kibbutznikim in shorts and sandals, soldiers with weapons slung over their shoulders, tanned women, bright-faced children, all waiting behind barricades for arriving passengers. Warm, scented air brushed against her, stirring memories. She had been to Israel twice before, each time interviewed, written about, lionized. Despite her hawkish politics, the leftist secular Israeli intelligentsia could not get enough of her. Now, in her season of drought, she felt herself a fraud and dreaded the prospect of media pursuit.

Beyond the barricades, a portly, middle-aged man stepped out of the crowd and moved quickly toward her. Shaul Hofshi, professor of Hebrew literature, an old friend. Small gray eyes, jowly features, moist lips. Baggy light-brown trousers, old sandals, a short-sleeved white shirt. Patches of pale skin in the open slits between the buttons of the straining shirt; deep crease lines radiating along the front of the trousers from the crotch. He greeted her effusively, took her valise, asked how was the flight, said how good it was to see her again, surely she must be exhausted, they would go immediately to Jerusalem and get her settled in her room in the university faculty club so she could get some rest, they would talk in the car about her schedule, the conference, interviews, meanwhile please to wait here a few minutes, he would be right back with the car, please not to move.

He left her alone with her valise and overnight bag at a turbulent curbside. Behind her swirled the dense noisy crowd talking the language she did not know. The faces of all the world's Jews seemed gathered here. Cars clogged the road. Some stopped where she stood, loaded up with passengers and baggage, and pulled away. She strained for a glimpse of Shaul's old Renault. The low bright afternoon sun stabbed her tired eyes. Diesel fumes thickened the air. A hot wind blew up her dress and between her legs. She smelled the sweat that rose from her and felt on her tongue the sour taste of desperation. She asked herself: What am I doing here? Why have I come?

Shaul Hofshi loaded her bags on to the back seat; the trunk was full of 'family things'. He drove the car out of the airport and immediately made a wrong turn. Instead of the road to Jerusalem, they were traveling in the opposite direction, toward Tel Aviv.

'I am embarrassed,' Shaul said. 'I have been on this road a hundred times, a thousand times, I am never before lost. What is the matter with me today?' There was sweat on his long upper lip and round smooth pink cheeks and high balding forehead. 'We must get off this road.'

I. D. sat beside him gazing out the window at the wide black asphalt road and the tall large-leaved palm trees and the green carpeting of the cultivated fields. She closed her eyes to shut out the rush of wrong road.

Shaul said, 'This is ridiculous, this is absurd.' He swung off at the next exit, drove confusedly through a stop sign, and followed road signs to Rehovoth, going south now instead of east. I. D. surveyed the unfamiliar road, feeling the hot fabric of the seat on her back and bottom. An overhead sign to Jerusalem suddenly appeared. 'We are saved! The redeemer has come to Zion!' Shaul exulted, making the turn.

They rolled along the wide curving mountain road to the holy city.

In his splendid Viennese-accented English, Shaul talked about The Situation. It was terrible, simply terrible. Jews weren't cut out to be occupiers, occupation was out of fashion in post-modern Western civilization, there would eventually have to be some sort of accommodation, territory for peace, but there was no one on the other side to talk to. With regard to the conference, today was Thursday, tomorrow and the weekend were for rest and recovery from jet lag. Then there would be a full day of papers on Sunday, to be delivered in the holy tongue by clever professors. On Monday noon there would be a visit to the great man's Jerusalem home, and, in the late afternoon, an official reception by the mayor of the city. Tuesday evening, three papers in English, I. D. Chandal's to be the last of the conference, her words thereby garlanding the proceedings and, by implication, the department and the university with an aura of international respectability. There would, of course, be the usual phalanxes of photographers, journalists, television people, critics, and cranks.

Would her paper be available in advance? he asked.

She didn't think so, she said.

What was she planning to do for Shabbat? he asked.

She had a friend with whom she would stay, she answered.

In Jerusalem?

Yes.

The road levelled after a lengthy climb and they entered the city. It lay tiered upon its hills, glowing pink in the setting sun. Pedestrians crowded the sidewalks: men and women in ordinary garb, bearded Hasidim in dark hats and long dark coats, Arabs in flowing robes and kafeeyas, uniformed soldiers with weapons: a bazaar of bodies in constant motion. Traffic choked the streets. The tumid mixture of diesel fumes and desert heat came thickly to her nostrils. But the city caressed her softly, whispering, as it had in the past. Visions floated before her eyes: kings and sages, poets and lawgivers, armies and conquests, centuries of walls upon walls, emblazoned towers and ornamented minarets: a city of a million tales. Whatever the coarse and bloodied politics of the land, Jerusalem was for her eternally graced by a serene and unsubstantial reality. How many books of folklore had she read about this city? Aberrant, unearthly things happened to people in Jerusalem. She gazed out the open window of the Renault. A cat lay dead near the curb on Herzl Boulevard, crushed by the wheels of a car. She chose not to see it.

'I will bring you straight to your room,' Shaul said, 'and then I will leave you so you can rest. At eight o'clock, a member of the English faculty will take you out for supper in a nice restaurant. Acceptable?'

'Perfectly acceptable,' I. D. said.

The room was small, cell-like: pale-green walls, dark-tiled floor, sealed windows. A bed, a desk, a lamp, a bureau. A tiny bathroom. The walls, bare. She lay on the bed and listened to the air-conditioner. It rattled and vibrated and shifted with a thudding whine into its cooling mode, then after a while shifted back to its windy roar. She had tried switching it off: the room became a cauldron. Switched on, the air-conditioner filled the room with the clank and grind of a New York subway train. Between cauldron and train, she chose train. Her heart pounded, her eyes ached. She lay very still on the bed, hungry, unable to sleep, her nerves overloaded. The grit of travel clung to her despite a shower and change of clothes. Those sleepless hours on the jetliner. She had sat up all night reading a novel by

[83]

the dead Israeli author. At the end of World War I, a man arrives by train on a brief visit to a ravaged Eastern European town, and finds himself lost in its nightmares. Long authorial meanderings, interior monologues, symbol-laden characters and events. Fretful Hasidim wandering up and down the aisles of the aircraft; rowdy teenagers in the tail section. At times the Hasidim seemed to enter the novel; the novel became the inside of the aircraft.

Lying on the bed, her hand over her eyes, I. D. began impulsively to fashion and discard sentences. Figures of speech fluttered about, phrases, clauses, sentences: a street-language enallage; a choked-off aposiopesis; an inexpressible aporia. All ascended, flitted, sailed through the air, became quickly threadbare, and tumbled into the scrap heap of discarded images and words that littered her recent life. She had taken the baroque sentence to its rococo heights; emptied the well. What now? An asyndeton flew into her mind: I wish, I writhe, I write. She gazed upon it, cringed at its fatuousness, and shut it from her mind. She slipped into a vision of Virginia Woolf walking into the river Ouse, her pockets laden with stones. Water reaching to her ankles, her knees, her thighs; water seeping into her crotch and over her breasts; water lapping at her throat. The air-conditioner thudded into its cooling whine. I. D. fell into a restive half-sleep.

Promptly at eight o'clock the telephone on the night table rang twice. I. D. sat bolt upright on the edge of her bed, not knowing where she was. The telephone rang again, shrill in the tiny room.

It was the person from the English literature department, a woman, come to fetch her. Was I. D. ready for a bite of supper in a nice restaurant?

She washed her face in the cramped bathroom, stared at herself in the mirror. Pudgy sallow features, bulbous nose, darkly circled brown eyes; the face of a waitress, a union organizer, a bus driver. She dried her face, put a touch of rouge to her cheeks, and went from the room, pulling the door shut and turning the key.

The woman from the English department was about ten years younger than I. D., tall and thin, her straight raven hair in bangs over her narrow forehead. She looked keenly at I. D. as they shook hands in the faculty club lobby: her eyes mirrored clearly the envy academicians often unveil in the presence of the working artist. She spoke English with a pronounced South African accent. 'How very good to meet you. An admirer for years. Your collection of stories, *Sacred and Profane*, simply marvelous.' Her specialty, she informed I. D., was American literature; her doctorate, on disequilibrium in William Faulkner. From Oxford. I. D. sat cramped in the front seat of her Volkswagen, listening to her talk, as they drove out of the university and through quiet streets to an outdoor café in the Rechavya section of the city.

Did I. D. know about the leftist poet who had cancelled a poets' conference he had organized in Jerusalem? the woman asks.

I. D. did not know. 'When was this?'

'About a week or so ago.'

Shaul had said nothing. A canny Viennese, he knew to stay away from political wrangles with I. D. Chandal. In certain intellectual Israeli circles, she was considered a fascist: Give back nothing; better to fight them in the Territories than on your doorstep, was her position. 'Why did he cancel it?'

'He said this is an immoral state unworthy of the presence of poets.'

'Who is this poet?' I. D. asks after a moment.

The woman mentions a name unfamiliar to I. D. 'A great poet. But politically a child.'

They are sitting in the café over a late supper. I. D. breathes deeply of night air still faintly edged with the desert odors of the

[85]

day. Nearby is the residence of the Prime Minister, with a police guard outside. What does he think of these days as he tries to sleep?

'I live here now seventeen years,' says the woman. 'For the first time, I'm afraid.'

'Afraid? Of what?'

'Of massacre. If they stop throwing stones and start using guns.'

'Won't the Army go in with force?'

'That's precisely what I mean,' the woman says. 'Massacre. On both sides.'

They eat awhile in silence.

'When it first started,' the woman says, 'people from Tel Aviv wouldn't go to Jerusalem. They thought it was raining stones in Jerusalem.'

'How much more quiet than this can the city be?'

'Less than a kilometer or two from here they throw stones.'

A vague clutch of fear like a heartskip. She stares into a night street empty of traffic and pedestrians. 'Really?'

'I had dreams they would break into my home at night. Amos Oz nightmares. Displaced fantasies. You know what I mean. Sex and things. You know.'

'How long do you think it will go on?'

The woman shrugs. 'Both sides are paralyzed politically. There are no new ideas anywhere. Who knows how long it will go on?' She chews thoughtfully on a piece of bread, swallows, turns brightly to I. D. 'Enough about politics. Shall we talk of happier things? Tell me what you're working on these days.'

Deposited later that night on the sidewalk in front of the wide stone stairs of the faculty club, I. D. stands watching the receding lights of the Volkswagen. A black jewelled sky rests like the inside of a colossal dome over the hills and valleys of the city. The university buildings, spread across the valley, are dark and silent. Distantly, a dog barks, and there is a brief scurrying nearby: cats moving restlessly among bushes and stones. I. D. shivers in night air still faintly viscous with the scents of the desert. Her eyes, heavy; in her temples, a sudden throb; in her ears, a brief ringing. She knows the signs: fatigue, stress, confusion. Back to the room and the clamorous black box of the air-conditioner. Narrow bed. Tiny, cramped desk. Dim lights. What time was it now in New York? Three in the afternoon?

She entered the dimly lit deserted lobby of the faculty club, walked along the narrow hallway, and came into the room. The air was hot and stifling: dry fingers suddenly in her throat and nostrils, choking her. She hurried to the window and turned on the air-conditioner and stepped back as the machinery came to life and hot air shot out.

She sat on the bed and then at the desk and then went to the bathroom and back to the bed. The air in the room turned quickly cool and moist, but she sensed it rimmed by a cloud of heat that threatened to penetrate the walls. She removed her dress and lay on the bed and then sat up and took off her bra and panties and lay back again. Quickly, the cotton spread felt hot and coarse beneath her, and she folded it back and rolled down the blanket. Her long flat pale breasts flopped about as she moved: desiccated extensions of her aging flesh, dry as the desert was dry, as the thrown stones were dry, as her writing was dry. She had the unfamiliar sensation of herself as oddly jellylike, a non-vertebra. She lay back on the bed, uncovered, her arms over her eyes, her knees lifted. Heat rose from her flesh, her throat quivered. The air-conditioner shifted with a heavy thud to cooling; the walls of the room vibrated. Her raised knees pale pink hills on the white sheet, the mound at the juncture now visible, its hair dense and curled, still the light-brown color of her youth. She touched herself lightly then, fingering the moist rise, and was gone for some while. Then she lay languid, the sheen of sweat wondrously cool on her face and forehead. Eyes closed, she remembers the hills of Daphne outside Antioch in southern Turkey that she once climbed with her husband: waterfalls gushing from the stony hillside and streaming across the rocky earth. Green shrubs, luxuriant trees, a cool wind moving like a silken veil across the face of the hill, stirring the leaves. Easy to imagine Daphne worshipped there in pagan times; easy to envisage nymphs and naiads and dryads gamboling there. Good stones, gentle stones, stones wet with sparkling streams and glistening in the sunlight that filters through the leaves.

I. D. reads and dozes and wakes and reads again. She goes to the bathroom and urinates and stands naked before the mirror over the sink. This loose-skinned dumpy hag staring at her! *Who is she?* The air-conditioner thumps into its cooling mode, and she slumps against the sink, startled by the feel of the cold porcelain upon her inflamed skin. I. D. Chandal. Yes. *Where?* Jerusalem. Oh, yes. City of – what? Stones raining upon soft flesh. Truncheons flailing young skin. Visions of tumescent olive-skinned youths lurking in the shadows outside her window. She has been in this land less than a day but already feels three thousand years old.

Returning to the bed, she lies down naked upon the sheet and takes up the book of stories by the great man. She tries to read and is soon asleep. Faces appear to her, worn and deeply wrinkled, hardened to leather by the beating sun. Narrow pastel-colored houses, and sun-bleached streets, and nearby a vast expanse of heaving sea. As if through the wall a dog bounds suddenly into the room, huge, black, and ugly; it stares at her out of red-rimmed eyes, its breath hot – and then turns and lopes away. She lies asleep, terrified. Somewhere along the edge of the room hovers the figure of a short portly man in a fedora, dimly visible in the region of heat along the walls. I. D. wakes and shivers and covers herself with the blanket and reads again.

It is nearly four in the morning, Jerusalem time. She will soon be asleep and will sleep late, probably till noon. Then she will eat and later pack a bag and call for a taxi and go to spend Shabbat with her friend. They'll have a good dinner together in her friend's apartment and then sit around and talk or maybe go to a party. Her friend works in the Ministry of Interior, and she'll get the latest information from her about the uprising. Wait one moment, *wait*: Has she phoned her friend to let her know she'll be with her for Shabbat? She *must* have phoned her! *Her?* Wait one moment: Isn't her friend a *man?* How strange that she can't remember. Time enough to call when she wakes. Yes, soon she'll be asleep. But after some while, she is still awake. She reaches over and turns off the light on the night stand. She lies very still in the darkness, listening to the air-conditioner and waiting to fall asleep.

She sleeps until one in the afternoon. The floor maid tapping on her door wakes her. She has something to eat in the garden restaurant, then sits at the table, reading stories by the great man. How to get into him? Modernist, medievalist, elusive. 'Allusive, elusive, illusive,' she murmurs. He seems located nowhere, in no culture solidly. True ambiguity. False ambiguity is humbiguity. She is still hungry and goes inside to the counter for another sandwich and coffee. Hunger and ambiguity equals fambiguity: starved by questions which leave you without answers. She sits reading, and when she glances again at her watch, is astonished by the lateness of the hour. She returns to her room, hurriedly packs her overnight bag, taking along the great man's book of stories, and phones for a taxi.

In the corridor, she turns the key twice and yanks the handle up and down. The door to her room is securely locked.

She walks along the corridor to the entrance hall and the front door. Through the turretlike windows that look out on to the open-air interior garden comes the light of the afternoon sun.

She pushes down on the metal handle of the wide front door and pulls inward. The door does not open. Turning the button on the lock, she pulls again on the door. It remains closed.

Save for the woman caretaker, she is now alone in the faculty club building, everyone has gone off for Shabbat. How is it she has been locked into the building?

Standing in front of the closed door and holding in her hand her overnight bag, she listens for a moment to the silence in the building, and thinks, The taxi will come, and I won't be outside, and the driver will leave.

She goes to the phone on the reception desk, puts down the overnight bag, and dials 22.

The phone returns no sound of ringing. She hangs up and dials again. Then once more. No ringing, no response.

She returns the phone to its cradle, picks up the overnight bag, and walks to her room. A gauze curtain now hangs between herself and the world, and she has some difficulty unlocking the door. With the air-conditioner off, the room is hot and vaguely fetid. Seated on the edge of the bed, she dials 22 and hears the phone ring twice.

A woman answers. I. D. says this is room 6, the door to the building doesn't open. After a brief pause, the woman says she doesn't understand, what door doesn't open? I. D. says the front door, it's jammed or the lock is broken, it won't open, and the taxi will leave if she isn't outside when it arrives. The woman says she will come immediately, and hangs up.

I. D. puts down the phone, goes into the bathroom, washes

her hands and face. She locks the door to the room and walks along the corridor and down the stairs with her overnight bag.

The woman stands in front of the entrance door in a yellow cotton bathrobe and open-backed slippers. She holds the robe to her throat with the stubby fingers of her left hand.

I. D. says, 'Please excuse me for disturbing you on such an afternoon.'

The woman says, 'It is all right, you did not disturb me, what did you say is the matter?'

I. D. says, 'The door won't open, the taxi will be coming any minute, and the driver won't wait for me.'

'But the lock is right here,' says the woman.

'I tried the lock,' I. D. explains.

'You turned it?'

'Yes. And the door would not open.'

The woman leans forward, twists the round metal knob of the lock, and pushes lightly with her right arm against the door.

I. D. watches the door swing open.

A desert wind blows the musky scents of flowers and shrubs into the entranceway. I. D. hears herself say, 'Thank you,' and does not look at the eyes of the woman.

The woman says, 'May you have a day of complete rest,' and goes off.

Carrying her overnight bag, I. D. steps outside. Behind her, the door closes with a faint click.

She stands on the landing of the front stairs. A huge sun hangs over the baking stone hills, flattening distances, etching clearly the rectangular outlines of houses, the stepped rises of hillside fields, the green of faraway pines. She breathes in the hot odors of the earth, feels the ache in her temples and the clamminess between her legs. How did she forget that the front door opened outward? How does one forget something like

[91]

that? Clearly she was not well. A summer flu? Something far more serious? What? She sits down on the graystone bench near the front stairs.

The bench is in the shade. She has on her dark glasses, but even so the sunglare on the asphalt road torments her eyes. She hears a car and sees a small red Renault turn into the road and go past the faculty club. An unease like the first flush of an illness comes upon her. She puts a hand to her forehead; it comes away wet.

She thinks to go back inside and call the taxi company again. But they were always busy this time of the week and she would have to call them a number of times to get through, and what if the taxi came while she was inside and the driver saw she wasn't there and drove off?

She goes over to the curb and gazes up and down the road. Standing in the sunlight, she feels immediately the sun burning her face. She returns to the bench and sits down.

She waits what seems to her to be a long time. As she waits, she senses all around her, from the tawny hills and the deserted roads and the empty stone buildings of the university and the tall cypresses and shade trees – she senses a stillness that is like an expectation, a taut hovering upon some threshold of long-ing. She looks again at her watch.

An old Mercedes turns into the road and stabs the silence twice with its horn. Quickly, I. D. picks up her overnight bag and steps into the sunlight.

The taxi speeds through the campus gate and on to Rupin Street. Gazing at the road through the rear window, I. D. suddenly realizes that she may not be correctly remembering the address of the person with whom she is to stay. The address is in her notebook, which is in her room inside the large valise. She should have looked at it again before leaving. She asks herself, What is the matter with me? First the silliness with the door, and now the address. Suppose I've given the driver the wrong address and he drops me there and takes off. I don't even have a token to call for another cab.

She looks out the side windows of the taxi at the hot and deserted streets. Late Friday afternoon in Jerusalem: everywhere silent sand-colored stone houses; the few cars on the roads nearly all taxis. Long hard-edged shadows lie across the streets mottled with dark purples and blues and blackish reds. As the taxi turns a corner, the side where I. D. is sitting catches the full force of the sunlight, and she shuts her eyes against the sudden piercing explosion of flaring incandescence.

The taxi turns off the boulevard and enters a neighborhood of narrow hilly streets and low sand-colored stone houses.

The driver glances at I. D. in the rear view mirror and says, 'What's the address again?'

I. D. hesitates, trying to remember it as she wrote it in the notebook.

'Hallo,' the driver says. 'Madam. The address.'

She repeats the street name and number. Was she confusing the number with that of the house in which she stayed briefly twenty-five years earlier before the city was united? How tranquil the city was that year!

'I think that's right near here,' the driver says. Then, 'You are in Jerusalem long?'

'Two days.'

'You fell into hot weather.'

'How do I lower this window?'

'I'm sorry. Kids unscrewed the handle. They have nothing to do, they turn wild.' He glances at her in the rear view mirror. 'So what do you think?'

'About what?'

'The Situation.'

'I'm not an expert.'

'In this, no one is an expert. Not even the government. You're from America.'

'Yes.'

'I decided I go to America. My wife say to me, "America not for us. A crazy place. Drugs and killing." I tell her, "You see too much American movies. Anyway, in America drugs and killing, here stones and killing. When I have enough money, I go to America." She say she don't want to go. I say when I have enough money, I go, she want to stay here, she can stay here. I tired of war and more war and stones and bombs. I look for something new.' He is craning his neck, scanning the houses on the right side of the road. 'This is the street, all right. What's the number again?'

She tells him.

'Ah, we pass it,' the driver says, suddenly braking, sending her lurching forward. He shifts into reverse, drives backward along most of the block, and stops. 'It should be here.'

I. D. pays the driver, climbs carefully out of the taxi, and reaches in for her overnight bag. The taxi pulls away and speeds around a corner.

I. D. stands alone on the hot silent street.

She is looking for number 7. She sees number 5. She picks up the bag and walks up the street. The house next to number 5 is number 9.

She walks back to number 5. It is a three-story house with front porches and a wide wooden entrance door. Cats lounge among the garbage bins.

The sun throws a blaze of light and heat across this side of the street. She squints as she looks at the number 5 on the white metal plate above the entrance door. Then she walks again up the street. The adjacent house has four stories, wide stone porches, and a closed entranceway over which is an address plate that reads: 9.

She sets down the bag, shades her eyes with her right hand, and gazes up and down the street.

The porches are deserted. Across the street a dog saunters by and disappears into the shadows between two houses. She will have to ring someone's bell and ask about number 7. People are in the shower, or getting dressed, or napping, or reading the weekend newspapers. Ring a bell and ask where it is and if it turns out to be right in front of your eyes, you will feel again as you felt when the woman in the faculty club lightly pushed against the entrance door.

The sun stings her eyes. Heat shimmer rises from the sidewalk. The azure sky is cloudless, the air faintly washed in a burning yellow haze. Twice she walks back and forth between number 5 and number 9. Then she stands in the sunlight beside her overnight bag. Behind her, the sun glows the color of blood above the rim of the far hills.

For a long moment she closes her eyes. When she opens them, she notices a man entering the street from the far corner below. Alongside him walks a middle-sized, short-haired dog, pale-brown in color and of an undetermined breed, the sort that roams wild in the desert and runs in scavenger packs in the early hours of the morning through the city's silent streets.

The man and the dog approach and proceed to pass her as if she is not there.

I. D. says to the man, 'Excuse me, please. Are you by any chance familiar with this neighborhood?'

The man stops and gazes at her. He seems mildly startled to have been addressed. The dog comes to a halt and growls.

'Be still,' the man says softly to the dog, who becomes

instantly docile. Then he says to I. D., 'This neighborhood I
know very well, yes.'

'Where is number 7?'

'Number . . . ?'

'Number 7.'

'Ah, number 7. Which number 7 do you wish?' the man asks.

The sun is shining directly upon his face. He appears to be in
his late sixties or early seventies, with round smooth florid
features, a large beaked nose, sharp blue eyes, and a small
straight mouth slightly downturned at the corners. He wears a
lightweight gray suit, a pale gray tie over a white shirt, and a
dark-gray, wide-brimmed summer hat.

'I don't understand,' I. D. says.

'Exactly which number 7 do you wish?' the man asks. His
English is accented, like the English of I. D.'s dead father who
was born near Lvov in the region of Galicia in eastern Poland.

'I'm looking for the house with the number 7.'

'Ah, the house that is number 7,' the man says. His soft voice
is shaded with a faint tone of amused superiority. The dog rises
and begins to sniff about. The man says, 'Behave yourself and
do not disturb the lady. Come here and sit. Sit. Good.' Then he
says to I. D. with a pale smile, 'May I ask from where are you?'

'From New York.'

'Ah.'

'New York City.'

'Ah.'

'Manhattan.'

'You have a family?'

'A husband. A son. An ailing mother.'

'The husband does what?'

She tells him what her husband does.

'And the son?'

'The son is at Harvard. An undergraduate.'

'And you are in Jerusalem for what?'

She tells him why she is in Jerusalem. He listens intently, nodding.

'Hebrew you know?' he asks finally.

She shakes her head.

'You will write about this author, and you do not know Hebrew?'

'Well, I've written about Flaubert, and my French isn't that good. I've written about Primo Levi, and I don't know Italian.'

'I understand Joyce studied Norwegian in order to read Ibsen.'

'Joyce was . . . Joyce.'

'What you write is read?'

'There are those who are interested.'

'America never fails to astonish.'

'It's getting late. May I ask again where is the house with the number 7?'

'It is a problem, the number 7. I must deal with it, you see.'

'I don't understand.'

'There are many sevens. I must deal with that.'

'Many sevens?'

'Very many, yes.'

'I'm sorry, I don't understand.'

'Well, there are the seven days of creation and the seven days of the festivals and the seven heavens and the seven tales I once created without comprehending their meaning until it was explained to me by others. There are the seven ascents to the Sacred Presence and the seven hours of labor at my stand that I dedicate to the Holy One blessed be He every day. There are the seven who are my good friends and the seven with whom I quarrel. There are the seven I read when I was young, among them Hamsun and Dostoevsky and Balzac, and the seven I read when I was older, among them, Kafka and Freud and Hesse. There are the seven blessings of joy and the seven verses of mourning and the seven years you labored at your first great success and the seven months you labored at your first great failure. There are the seven months thus far of The Situation and the seven forests that are burning and the seventh hour of this day, when the sun sets, and the seventh year in the life of Balak, who sits here with uncharacteristic patience. And you seek the seven of the address. The seven of the address is a between-thing, and you will find it only if you look with care. It is not the one or the other, but *between* the two. You must *look* for it keenly. Well, now I must go. You are right, it is getting late. Come, Balak.'

I. D. stares at him uncomprehendingly. A car turns into the street. I. D. wonders if she should flag down the driver and ask for the address. The car goes by. She looks up the street and sees the man and his dog turn the corner and disappear.

She is alone again on the street.

She lets her eyes move carefully back and forth across the stones and shrubbery between the numbers 5 and 9. Then she sees the stairway.

It lies behind a cover of lantanas, the leaves drooping over the metal banister. You could not see it from the street unless you knew it was there or stood angled in a way that would let you glimpse the stone stairs through the tangle of branches and leaves.

She picks up the bag and begins to climb the stairs. The leaves form a cool green-shadowed bower. She comes to a landing that turns into a dirt path that passes in front of a kitchen and a bedroom. She goes on beneath full-leaved trees to more stairs and another landing. On the landing she looks toward the west where the sun now touches the hills: a huge red globe, the air around it white and pink, its light faintly dulled by dust and the smoke of a distant fire.

On the top landing she stops before a door. Attached to the door is a white ceramic tile with a flowery green border. In the center of the tile, in bright red, is the number 7.

She rings the bell and hears its soft music on the other side of the door: three chimes. She stands on the landing, waiting. Silence and the scents of myriad flowers fill the hot still air.

The knob turns and the door opens inward. Carrying her bag, I. D. steps inside.

The elderly man greets her with a cordial smile. He has removed his hat and in its place he wears a dark round velvet skullcap. The dog lies on the rug in the entrance hall, awake and wary but very still.

'This is the address you want?' the man asks.

THE
INDIAN MUTINY

Will Self

I killed a man when I was at school. I'm not just saying that, I really did. And you know the fact of it has eaten away at me for years. Even now, sitting in my office at the station, in the dead centre of a dead ordinary day, I get chilly and sweaty thinking about it.

It was a shit thing to do, a truly bad thing. When I was growing up – after it had happened – I didn't dwell on it that much. It wasn't as if I had beaten the back of his head in with a spade and watched his brains run out like grey giblets, or poisoned him so that he died kicking and thrashing, or stabbed him, shot him, or hung him ejaculating and shitting from a spindly tree.

Don't get me wrong – these aren't my imaginings. I don't visualize things like this. Like I say, when I was in my teens, my early twenties, I didn't think of it as actually murdering someone. I read my behaviour differently, innocently.

He was my history teacher, I was his pupil. He had a mental breakdown one day, actually in the class, while he was taking a lesson. He was hospitalized, but we heard that he killed himself a couple of weeks later. Killed himself by self-suffocation.

Years later I heard that what he had done was to shut himself in a tiny broom cupboard. He caulked up the cracks in the door. That's how he died, sitting in the close, antiseptic darkness. That's what triggered it, I suppose. Before that I might have suspected that I had more to do with his death than the other boys in 4b, but I didn't know. When I heard how he died I knew that I had killed him.

Soon after that the dreams came. The dreams where I'm

looking at the blade of the spade, or fastening the elasticated belt around his thick, red neck. It's astonishing how many different ways I've murdered Mr Vello in my dreams. Murdered him and murdered him and murdered him again. I'd say that while I've slept I've probably killed Mr Vello at least two thousand times. And you wanna know the really queer thing about it? Every time I do him, I do him in a fresh way – an original way.

Some of the ways that I've dreamt I killed Mr Vello are positively baroque. Like shredding his buttocks to a pulpy mass, my weapon a common cheese grater. Or like pulling his head off. Just pulling it right off and sort of de-coring his body. Really icky stuff. I'm glad I can't express this too well in words because it's worse than any special effect you've ever seen. I don't know where the dreams come from because I don't see the world that way. I've never watched an operation, or been in an abattoir. I don't go to horror movies. I've never even seen a dead person. So I just don't know I get all these vivid anatomical details.

Of course it's the guilt. I know that. I'm not stupid, far from it. I've got the real gift of the gab. I can talk and talk. That's what I do for a living: talk and talk. That's what the kids at school said about me, 'You can talk like a chat show host, Wayne,' that's what they said. And it was prophetic, because now I am a chat show host. I went straight from being a lairy kid to being a lairy adult. That's how I really killed Mr Vello of course, I killed him with my big mouth. I killed him by winding him up. Winding him up so tight that he shattered. He just shattered.

Yeah, I did him all right. But I can tell you I didn't do it all by myself. I couldn't have managed it without the Indian Army.

Mr Vello came to us as a supply teacher. He wasn't like the other teachers at the school. He didn't wear PVC car coats, or ratty corduroy jackets. He didn't speak with a Cockney accent, or try and speak with one. He didn't read the *Guardian*, or the novels of D. H. Lawrence. Mr Vello dressed like a retired Indian Army officer. I think that's how he saw himself.

He was a solidly plump Yorkshireman in his mid-fifties. He always dressed in a blue blazer with brass buttons – the York-shire County Cricket Club badge was on the breast pocket. Mr Vello combed his hair back tight over his scalp. He had been using Brylcream for so many years that the thin slick of his hair had become Brylcream-coloured. Mr Vello's face was moley rather than vulpine, but when he got angry, which he did with increasing frequency, his apparently friendly, diffident wrin-kles seemed to get smarmed back with his greasy hair.

With the benefit of culpable hindsight I can place myself behind Mr Vello's metal-framed spectacles and picture class 4b as it must have appeared to him when he first swung back the big wooden door and walked in on us.

Simmo was doing his drawing pin trick. This was a bogus bit of fakirism whereby he placed three drawing pins on top of a desk and put his fat white hand over them. He then asked another boy to stamp on the back of his hand. On this occasion Simmo got it wrong – just as Mr Vello walked into the room he screamed and held up his hand. The three drawing pins were deeply embedded.

'What's all this?' said Mr Vello, setting a pile of textbooks down on the teacher's desk.

'Please, sir,' gurgled Simmo (blood was beginning to flow), 'please, sir, I've hurt my hand.'

'Nonsense, boy,' said Mr Vello. 'Now sit down and shut up . . . All of you: sit down, shut up and pay attention.'

But we didn't. We never did. We just went on: flicking rubber bands; chasing one another around the desks; bashing and shouting. The majority, that is. But really there were three distinct minorities in class 4b: the Jews, the Gentiles and the

Asians. 4b was a bipartisan culture however and power derived solely from the antagonism between the Jews and the Gentiles. We formed two gangs and called ourselves respectively 'The Yids' and 'The Yocks'.

The Asian boys were different. They were all first-generation immigrants, mostly West African Asians, expelled from Uganda and Kenya, but some Punjabis and Pakistanis as well. It could have been this factor alone, or perhaps it was because Asian families have a more pronounced tradition of respect for pedagogues, but none of the Asian boys were indisciplined or cheeky. On the other hand they didn't exactly stick together. They certainly didn't all sit together in the classroom. It was as if they had conspired together to be unobtrusively unobtrusive. I reckon Mr Vello picked up on this immediately. Because it was the Asian boys who stopped buggering about first. They all sat down in their desks and got their books out.

Mr Vello saw the rest of us, immediately, for what we were: time-servers; time-wankers; ignorantly urbane boys – full of nasty decadences. The doomed scurf on the last polluted wave of our culture. He said as much, or rather shouted it.

'You boys are ignorant,' he shouted, 'ignorant of discipline.' He walked up and down the classroom batting the backs of heads with practised swipes of his wooden ruler. We yowled and yammered like the Yahoos we were. 'But it isn't your fault, you live in an undisciplined society and you are subjected to a banal cultural babble. You would do well to observe these Indian boys. They at least have been subjected in the more recent past to the rigours and responsibilities of imperial rule. Isn't that right, boy?' Mr Vello stopped by Jayesh Rabindirath, a thick oaf who was heavily mustachioed at fourteen.

'Err . . . yes, sir. I suppose so.'

Mr Vello tried to teach us. He tried for weeks. But he just couldn't hack it. Adolescent boys sense weakness in a teacher and go for it like piranhas sporting in offal. I think that in a quieter school, some nice private joint where the kids were better behaved, Mr Vello would have been OK. But at Creighton Comprehensive he didn't have a chance.

I think he was overwhelmed by the militancy of our philistinism, the utter failure of our didactic urge. Naturally we played up to this – me in a particular. It took only four maladministered lessons for the situation to deteriorate to such an extent that the poor man couldn't even talk for sixty seconds without being importuned by a battery of grubby paws, stuck out straining from the shoulder, at angles of forty-five degrees. 'Please, sir! Please, sir! Ple-ease, sir!' we all chorused, but as soon as he paid us any mind we would come up with some absurd request ('Please sir, may I breathe?'), our subservience a grotesque parody of his assumed authority. Or if, in the course of attempting to instruct us, he managed to shout out a question, we would vie with one another to produce the most facile, the most patently weak, the most irrelevant answer.

I think I managed the worst example of this fairly early on. Mr Vello was attempting to discourse on the Crimean War; back to the class, he mapped out the battlefield at Balaclava with a series of mauve chalk strokes. We had all fallen silent, the better to stand on our desks and wigglingly shimmy our contempt for him. Without bothering to turn he flung over his shoulder: 'Why were the Russian batteries positioned here?'

I came back triumphantly (God, have I ever been funnier?): 'Because that's where the little diagram said they should be positioned.' We all fell about. I got eighteen consecutive detentions. God, how we (and me in particular) loved it when he got worked up. It was so comic, there was something cartoony about the colour contrast between his blue, blue blazer and his red, bursting, humiliated face. Rebellion was in the air.

It was during the lesson after that that Mr Vello first announced the establishment of the Indian Army. 'Now then, boy-yz!' He thwacked his desk with his ever-handy ruler to give his words emphasis.

'Now then, boy-yz!' we all chorused back, thwacking our desks with our rulers. Things really had got that bad. Worse still, we all managed a pretty fair imitation of Mr Vello's idiosyncratic accent and enunciation. This was marked by a weird alternation in pitch between the swooping vowels of Yorkshire and the clipped consonants of received pronunciation. We were all pretty good at doing Mr Vello, but I was the best.

'Now then, boy-yz!' he came at us again. 'I have no patience any more with your in-disci-pline. None at all. I have noticed that your Indian colleagues maintain a healthier respect for authority than the rest of you, so I am going to adopt my own Martial Races policy.'

He got all the Indian boys to stand up and then he lined them up in the aisle in order of height. Jayesh Rabindirath at the front, behind him Dhiran Vaz, behind him Krishna Patel and so on, all the way down to the minuscule Surrinyalingam (no one ever knew his first name), a tiny blackened block of a boy, who wasn't an Indian at all but a Tamil – however, Mr Vello chose to ignore this fine distinction.

'I commission all you Indian boyz into my Indian Army.' He paced the next aisle, ruler on one shoulder like an officer's swagger stick. 'It is no longer my task, but yours, to maintain ab-so-lute order amongst this miserable, unlettered rabble . . .' As he spoke, my attention sideswiped out the window. A bus had pulled up and shook in mechanical ague by the concrete bus shelter. I could see fat old women coming out of the library across the road from the school and donning plastic rain hats. Life seemed to be proffering a teasing and perhaps crucial juxtaposition. I raised my arm. Mr Vello whirled on me. 'Yes, Fein?'

'Please, sir . . .'

'Yes, boy?'

'Please, sir, I want to join the Indian Army.'

'Don't be bloody stupid boy. Enlistment in the Indian Army is open only to boys of Indian descent. You, Fein, are of Semitic descent, you are a Levantine not an Aryan, therefore you shall not be called to the Colours.'

'Or the coloureds . . .' Simmo sniggered in the corner.

'But, sir, Mr Vello sir,' I kept on at him, 'my dad says we're Ashkenazi Jews, not Sephardim. He says we aren't really Semites at all.'

And this was true. My father had a touch of the Mr Vellos about him as well, a fondness for the *Daily Telegraph* (ironed) and village cricket. A relentless autodidact, he had been much taken by Arthur Koestler's theory that the Ashkenazi were in fact the descendants of the Scythian Khazaks, Turkic tribesmen who had converted to Judaism in the seventh century. Dad discoursed on this in the garden of an evening, smoking a briar pipe (his plumed flag of utter assimilation).

'Oh, and what are you if you're not a Semite?'

'I'm an Aryan, sir. My ancestors were Turkic tribesmen. My dad told me so, he's really interested in Jewish history.'

Mr Vello was nonplussed; he left off drilling the Indian Army and took to his desk where he cradled his head in his hands. And here's one of the sickest bits of this sick, sad tale, for Mr Vello really was a conscientious and unbigoted man – he was giving this matter of my lineage real thought, heavy consideration. The class was strangely silent. At length he stirred.

'All right, Fein, I'll make an exception as far as you are concerned, and in deference to your father's scholarship. You may join the Indian Army.'

So it was that I became an Indian Army soldier. What a soldier I was: relentlessly enforcing the order I had so recently been determined to disrupt. With my fellow soldiers I patrolled the aisles of the classroom swiping hair-covered collars with my ruler, confiscating fags and sweets, strutting my skinny, flannel-legged stuff. I exulted in the power. My sharp tongue grew sharper still. And was discipline imposed? Did Mr Vello's writ run class 4b? Did it hell. For in as much as I was an Indian Army soldier I was also its principle mutineer. I was the Fletcher Christian to Mr Vello's Captain Bligh ('Why did the mutineers throw away the breadfruit plants?' 'Please, sir. Please, sir.' 'Yes, Fein?' 'Because they were stale, sir!' Ha, ha, bloody ha).

Yes, it makes me sick now. Sick to think of it. Trim girlies come in and hand me things: write-ups and intelligence files on the guests I'm about to goose and humiliate, promote and patronize, fawn over and psychically fellate. That's my job. But if only I could get Mr Vello back, get him on the show. I'd recant, I'd apologize, I'd vindicate myself, and in doing so I'd make him whole again, make him live again, abolish the ghastly Vello golem that parades through my unconscious.

He got worse and worse. In one lesson he insisted on giving us a graphic description of the way he prepared his vegetable patch in the spring. In another he showed how, while on hazardous service during the latter war, he was taught to signal using a wind-proof lighter and a pipe. The Indian Army grew restless. It wasn't their idea, they just wanted to carry on being unobtrusively unobtrusive. After one particularly surreal lesson Dhiran Vaz and Suhail Rhamon got me in the corridor.

'You're a jerk, Fein,' said Vaz, as he gripped and twisted my collar. 'The poor man's having a breakdown, he's really going nutty and you're just goading him, making it happen. D'you like watching people suffer?'

'Yeah,' Rhamon concurred, 'we've had enough of this, we're going to talk to the headmaster . . .'

'Now hang on a minute, guys – guys.' I was emollient, placatory. 'I agree with you. I don't like it either, but I still think we should settle it ourselves. End the rule of the Indian Army in our own way.'

I won them round. I stopped them going to the head. I implied that if they did, the full weight of both the Yids and the Yocks would come down on them. They had no alternative.

The bubble burst the next Thursday. Mr Vello was ranting about the abandonment of the Gold Standard when I gave the signal. The soldiers of the Indian Army took up their pre-arranged positions: at the door, the windows, the light-switches. While they flashed the lights on and off I strode to the front of the class and deprived Mr Vello of his ceremonial ruler. He blinked at me in amazement, his eyes huge and bulbous behind the concave lenses of his glasses.

'What are you doing, Fein?'

I couldn't help giggling. 'This is it, sir,' I said. 'What we've been waiting for. It's the Indian Mutiny.'

Mr Vello looked at my horrible, freckly little face. His eyes swung around the room to take in the rebellious sepoys. He sat down heavily and began to sob.

He sobbed and sobbed. His heavy shoulders heaved and shook. His wails filled the room. When Simmo opened the door to the corridor they filled the corridor as well. Eventually the headmaster came with Mr Doherty, the gym teacher, and they led Mr Vello away, for ever.

So now you know how it was that I killed Mr Vello. Murdered him. You don't think that's enough? You think I'm being hard on myself? Children can be nasty after all – without meaning to be. But I meant to be, I really meant to be.

Last night I had one of my worst Mr Vello dreams yet. I was in Calcutta, it was 1857 – the Indian Mutiny was in full swing. Screaming fourteen-year-old sepoys broke into my villa and dragged me away. Their faces were distorted with blood lust and triumph. Dhiran Vaz hauled me along by the collar of my tunic. He and Rhamon took me and threw me in a cell, a tiny close cell, no more than forty feet square. And then they threw in the others, the other victims of the Mutiny: all my guests. All the guests I've ever had on Fein Time Tonight, one after another they came pressing into the cell, and each time another one entered there was another roar of approval from the crowd of sepoy classmates massed on the dusty parade ground outside. I was pressed into the wall, tighter and tighter. My eyes filled with sweat but my throat was parched. I got a pain as sharp as a stuck bone when I tried to swallow. My thirst was oppressive, I longed for something, anything to drink.

And then Mr Vello arrived. He was in his Yorkshire County Cricket Club blazer, as ever. The chat show guests passed him over their heads and then wedged him down beside me. He was still crying. 'Why did you do it, Fein?' he whimpered. 'Why did you do it?' And he was still whimpering when I buried my teeth into the leathery dewlap of his throat, still whimpering when I began to suck the life out of him.

GIRL DANCING

Tony Peake

Peter's progression from Hebden Bridge Grammar to the Royal College of Art was against the wishes of everyone except Miss Coveney who, as head of art at the grammar, was the only person to have a vested interest in his thus escaping his home town. For his mother the much vaunted letter from London (vaunted, that is, by Peter and Miss Coveney) was nothing less than the opening gambit in a game designed to cheat her of her son. For his father it was proof of economic lunacy and probable sexual deviancy: in Mr Gilling's eyes, painting (unless of houses) was neither a proper job, nor a job for a man. And as for seventeen-year-old Rita, with whom, in his parents' phrase, he'd been walking out, for her it signalled an end to the rather cautious and clumsy, but nonetheless pleasurable, exploration they'd begun of each other's bodies; an exploration which, she'd confidently expected, would eventually lead to a house of their own, a baby or two, and a satisfying succession of coffee mornings.

'Use your nous!' his father would rant, the two red spots on his cheeks igniting like flares in his anger and excitement. 'What money is there in painting? How does it pay the bills? And if you and Rita decide to tie the knot, then how the hell will it support you, eh? Just answer me that!'

'Never mind about Rita,' snapped his mother, who never had and didn't intend to start now. 'Do you know how far it is, London, by train? Or how expensive? What's wrong with Manchester, that's what I'd like to know? Or Leeds?' Having learnt from experience that it didn't do to be too specific with men in matters emotional, she let geography make the point for her: that a son's place was, if not actually in the home, then certainly in the immediate vicinity.

Rita, thankfully, was less articulate, although on the Saturday following his announcement, at their end-of-term dance, she nevertheless made her feelings perfectly plain by snivelling into his chest each and every time he hauled her on to the floor.

'No vision,' Miss Coveney said sharply when, a few days later, he sought her out and confided the trouble he was having squaring this familial disapproval with his own desire to be shot of Hebden Bridge even more quickly than the holidays would allow. 'A mean-spirited, low little place, richly deserving of the ugliness it spawns.' The window of her flat overlooked a regiment of houses marching in glum determination up the hill opposite to defend themselves against the bleak beginnings of the moor, and now, with a contemptuous sweep of her arm, she made as if to erase the sight.

'Oh, for a paintbrush!' she sighed dramatically. 'I'd just paint them out and start again. Oaks, don't you think, or elms, lots of elms, and on the ridge there, a girl, all by herself, just dancing, with only the trees for company.'

Hypnotized by the sweep of her arm, Peter felt the familiar rush of excitement and nausea she always engendered in him, a kind of guilty impatience to be free of himself, to be other than he was. Just as she, with her startling skirts and extravagant jewellery, her vivid make-up and shock of red hair, just as she seemed to have transformed herself from the merely earthbound into another, more vital element: a flame that burned with such intensity it threatened to ignite the town and reduce it to ash.

'I don't know, though,' he said warily. 'In a way I'm all they've got, and perhaps Dad's right, perhaps I should learn a trade.'

'And then?' challenged Miss Coveney. 'What then? You still have to ask the question: is it your life, or theirs?'

'Mine, of course. But they gave it to me.'

'Gave it, and therefore can't take it away. Life owes nothing, Peter, except to itself. Which is why, of course, they' – and here she gestured dismissively out of the window – 'are so afraid of it. Whereas you, my dear, you have talent, and a duty, therefore, to live life to the full, so that one day you can recreate it. You are their mouth, their ears, their eyes! And anyway, London! Just think! The galleries, the clubs, the people. You'll have such fun. You must find a room in Chelsea. It's the only place. Oh, you're going to love it, I just know you are!' And in her mounting excitement, she caught his hand and swung him round in such a sharp, quick circle he almost lost his balance.

In the event, though, and with an irony too perverse for him to relish, the London he encountered was to all intents and purposes nothing more than an obsequious reflection of Hebden Bridge. The year was 1965, and everywhere he turned, he came face to face not with novelty, but with a stylized version of the north. Hockney, the Beatles, Billy Liar: London's present was his past.

In his confusion and fright, he wrote to Miss Coveney, telling her dutifully that yes, he had found a room in Chelsea, but that no, he wasn't finding it fun. He tried to explain to her how out of step he felt; how, if he talked about beauty, the other students just laughed; or how, if he laughed himself at Hebden Bridge, or anything out of his past, they sprang to its defence; how realism reigned supreme, denying alternate ways of being.

I feel very isolated, he wrote. *Very on my own.*

Her reply, when it came, offered scant consolation. She said suitably soothing things, how settling in was always difficult, how the world was full of people with strange ideas; but it was ammunition he required, not placebos, and when she went on to enthuse about a new student who reminded her of him, then, with a sinking heart, he realized how little help he could expect from that quarter. He was, as he himself had said, out on his own.

And not just on his own, but also under attack; for what he hadn't told Miss Coveney was that Mr Trender, his tutor, didn't like his work.

'You can draw, all right,' he'd mutter in Peter's ear, his tobacco-tainted breath lending acrid texture to the harshness of his judgement, 'but draw what you see. It's too pretty-pretty, this. People want truth, not lies.'

At first Peter had tried to confront his inquisitor, had haltingly attempted, and in his own words where possible (he was beginning to distrust Miss Coveney's), to explain that for him reality wasn't all, or put another way, that there was more than one kind of reality, that what we see is only part of the picture. Mr Trender, however, just laughed.

'Look, lad, look! That's all an artist has to do: just look. Look around you, and then draw that. Leave theory to the critics.'

Easier said than done, though, especially as when he tried to follow Mr Trender's advice, the results were even less to his tutor's liking.

'What's this, then? If Jenny's arms were that long, we'd need season tickets to the Zoo in order to sketch her. Give here, look!'

And snatching the charcoal, Mr Trender would adjust the model's proportions with a quick slashing motion that seemed, to Peter, designed more to humiliate him than to correct the inadequacies of his draughtsmanship.

He began to lose confidence in his ability to draw, and half-way through the term, so badly had this loss of confidence affected his work, he was called before the head of department. No actual threats were made, the talk was all about potential – but even so, the message was clear; was encapsulated, in fact, in that single word: potential. The pupa was being reminded of its duty to pupate, and by a certain date, too: the end-of-term exhibition, to which all first-year students were expected to contribute a painting.

He could have fled, of course, tail between his legs, back to Hebden Bridge, where his parents and Rita were waiting; and where too, if she wasn't totally absorbed in her new pupil, he could have cried on Miss Coveney's shoulder. But tempting though that option was, something in him, not exactly a belief in himself, but a memory of how much less than himself he'd always felt in Hebden Bridge, determined him to stay and fight it out, to submit a painting for the exhibition that would, at a stroke, put paid to his tutor's scepticism.

He had no friends as such at the college, nor in the house where he rented his room, and because he didn't have the money to go drinking in the clubs that Miss Coveney had so vividly described – and where, though God knew how they afforded it, all the other students seemed to spend their time – what Peter took to doing of an evening, after he'd fried his supper on the ring in his room, was wrap himself in his coat and walk – walk endlessly and compulsively – from one end of Chelsea to the other, from the embankment to the Fulham Road, from Chelsea Bridge to Edith Grove, along streets whose rows of pretty houses were sealed by warmth and wealth from transients like himself, streets whose dark and derelict warehouses threw down the echo of his footsteps like a gauntlet, streets flanked by shops, streets flanked by parks, and down by Chelsea Wharf, streets that gave on to water and a bobbing flotilla of boats.

He seldom spoke to anyone in the course of these walks, except perhaps to point a stranger in the direction of some pub, or to smile approval on the antics of a dog, but then neither did he want to: the purpose of walking was to help map out a painting in his head, uncover some image that would validate his existence, would prove Mr Trender wrong.

Chelsea, however, for all its charms – or perhaps, he began to think wretchedly, because of them – refused to yield solutions, and finally, with just a week to go before the exhibition, he was forced to give up his walks and stay in his room, wrestling desperately with charcoal and paper, and beyond that his recalcitrant talent, which, if he'd ever had it, seemed to have deserted him with as much finality as he'd deserted Hebden Bridge.

On the Friday of that week, with a mere weekend between himself and certain ignominy, he sat down as usual after his fry-up and tried again to trick an image from the blank sheet of paper on his table. It was useless, though, and after a couple of increasingly pathetic attempts, he threw his charcoal to the floor, and snatching up his coat, fled into the soothing anonymity of Chelsea. With no idea of where he was heading, or why, he walked blindly up the King's Road, and then, turning northwards, began to zigzag at random from street to street, never looking where he was going, simply keeping on the move.

After an hour he started to tire, and as his pace slowed, so he began to take notice of his surroundings. He was in a road he didn't recognize, except generically, which is to say it was in no way different from any of the other Chelsea streets, except perhaps in the quality of its silence, which struck him as peculiarly intense. He paused, not so much to savour the silence as to verify it, and in so doing became aware, in the house to his left, that a young woman was standing at the downstairs window, staring into the street.

The house was set back from the pavement, and the square of yellow light that haloed the woman's head fell in an oblong bolt across the paved courtyard, trying for the street but not quite making it. He knew, though, that the woman could see him, because there was a street lamp to his right, and he was caught in the light from that.

Ordinarily, the fact that he could be observed would have

caused him to hurry on, but there was something oddly arresting about the way in which the young woman was looking at him. At once challenging and beseeching, her gaze demanded of him that he stop and watch her.

So he didn't move, and for a long while the two of them just stood there, staring at each other, until, very slowly, as if in a dream, she lifted first one arm, then the other, and began, ever so sensuously, to dance for him, to sway first to the left, then to the right, and then, with great assurance, to embark on a series of swooning pirouettes. She wasn't beautiful, or not in the accepted sense, she was too dumpy for that, and the haircut that framed her face was unnecessarily severe, but her movements were so supremely graceful, so confident and self-contained, and her gaze, as she danced for her audience of one, so wonderfully composed, that with each new movement she became that little bit more beautiful, that little bit more perfect. In the space of five minutes (less, even) she succeeded in returning colour and magic to his world, in making him forget his troubles, feel wanted again.

It was the most positive thing that had happened to him since his arrival in London – what was he saying, it was the only positive thing – and although he was scared that by moving he'd interrupt the spell, he was unable to prevent himself stepping off the pavement and into the oblong of light thrown from the window into the courtyard. To his surprise, the woman didn't falter in her dance, and after a moment, magnetized by her fluidity, he allowed himself to be drawn even closer, until, after a series of steps that in their own, hesitant way matched hers, he was standing just feet from the window.

It was only then, when, if it hadn't been for the glass, he could have put out a hand and brushed her cheek, that he saw why his approach had had no effect on her. She was blind, sealed off by her sightlessness not only from him, but from everything around her.

So unexpected was this revelation, and so cruelly shocking, that for a moment he was unable to move, and it was only when, after a final pirouette, she stopped her dance and turned from the window that anything approaching normality returned and he was able to breathe naturally again.

Still, though, he didn't move, not even when she glided to the door and left the room, for now a hot excitement had taken the place of shock, and suddenly he was devouring the details of the room, the mosaic of books in their alcoves on either side of the marble fireplace, the sagging sofa and matching armchairs, the prints on the wall, and, at the far end of the room, an open piano. Already titled, neatly framed by the window and vivid in his mind, was the picture he'd been so arduously seeking.

THE PICTURE

Shelley Weiner

'The steak's tough,' Alec grumbled. 'Again. It's the second time this week. I don't think I can eat it.'

'Sorry, Al.' Marcia, his wife, was deep into her calorie-counted salad platter. She glanced up momentarily, her eyelids burdened by the weight of a triple application of lash-enhancing mascara. Then she sighed exhaustedly, sinking her teeth into a stick of celery and frowning as she crunched and spoke. 'I did tell her. The maid. You know – Rosie. I've explained to her a hundred times how you like it. You must *beat* the master's steak, I said. I gave her that wooden hammer, the one with the spikes and told her *that's* the way the master wants it. Well beaten and well done. *Yes madam*. They always say yes madam. But what does that mean? You know how they are, never listening, only busy thinking about themselves. Al, I don't know why, but I have by doubts about Rosie. Mark my words, she won't last much longer . . .'

'OK, OK,' Alec sawed wearily at his steak. 'Look, Marce – I don't want to make a fuss. I've never made a fuss about my food. I mean, some men in my position would have lost their temper by now. But, well, under the circumstances, I suppose we have to be . . . careful with the girl. Can't afford to have her walking out at this point.'

This point. The point of no return. The eve of the arrival of his mother, who was coming to Cape Town to spend her last years with her only son the dentist. And why not, after all? Alec was prosperous, childless, the owner of a house quite large enough to absorb a little old lady with few possessions. Why not indeed? It was Alec's turn to sigh and frown as he forced his attention back to the unyielding slab of meat, stainless steel sawing and clinking against bone china, porcelain-capped molars grinding knots of gristle. Next thing he'd damage his bridgework and then where would he be? As it was, Milton and he were hardly managing to cope with the Christmas rush. Who'd have believed the number of people who insisted on celebrating the birth of their Messiah with a new crown or a fresh set of dentures or some renovated root canals? Shouldn't complain though. He surveyed the opulence of their ranch-style residence with its atrium, four reception rooms and all mod cons. There was profit in teeth. No doubt about it. Plenty, plenty. Enough for him to expect a decently cooked piece of steak at the very least.

'What time's her plane expected?'

'Hmm?'

Alec looked across the table. Marcia'd had her hair done. Dark copper curls cascaded down her neck, framed her perfectly made-up face and sprouted tendrils that licked the neck of her designer track suit in a way that was rarely permitted to him these days. Those damn useless fertility treatments had really knocked her libido. But, *man,* she looked good. Good enough to . . .

'Your mother.' A vertical line creased the well-tended space between her eyes. Marcia was not content. 'When's she due to arrive?'

He gathered his rampant thoughts and brushed a fly off his head and felt the December heat and the sparseness of his hair and wondered if a toupee would make him look younger and what his mother would think when she saw him. His mother.

Alec's stomach tightened. He pushed his plate aside. Marcia was chasing a recalcitrant chunk of cottage cheese with her fork. 'Over my dead body,' she'd sworn fiercely when the letter had arrived. And who could blame her? Zelda was ill, old, disappointed, disapproving and dying and asking to stay for as long as it took. After several appeals to Marcia's finer feelings (by way of three items of designer apparel, four ounces of French perfume and five days at a health farm), she had grudgingly conceded that 'the old cow' could be given a room as long as she didn't expect her daughter-in-law to alter her lifestyle for her.

'I will *not* lose touch with my friends,' she'd said defiantly – as though Alec had proposed placing his wife on twenty-four-hour mother alert. 'Look what happened to Nettie Lewis after her hysterectomy. She'd been out of action for six weeks – that was all, six weeks. And by the time she tried to get into the swing of things again she'd been quite forgotten. Husband having it off with her best friend, name off the duplicate bridge challenge list, maid pregnant, garden boy in jail. She may as well have left town. Might as well have been dead. She couldn't help it though. An operation's an operation. But I'll tell you one thing, Alec, I won't risk anything for your mother. Not a thing. She's always hated me, so why should I do anything for her now?'

'No, Marce. You're wrong.' He'd tried his best to placate her. He had been trying for fifteen years. 'It's not that she dislikes you. She was just ... disappointed. That's all. She'd set her heart on having a Jewish daughter-in-law. But she's accepted you now. Look – she even sends you birthday cards.'

Marcia had sniffed dismissively.

'Honestly, Marce,' Alec had said, struggling to keep his voice under control. He hated confrontations. 'I promise she won't be any trouble. I'll speak to Rosie. Get her to understand that looking after the old lady will be *her* responsibility. Perhaps give her a bonus or something – fifteen rand, maybe. You'll see. It'll be OK. Truly.'

She hadn't looked convinced and he had worried, when he allowed himself to think about it, how the arrangement would work out and whether he could do anything to prevent his mother coming. He loved her, naturally, but . . . Anyway, it was too late to change plans now. Zelda was on her way.

'The plane's expected around two,' he said, replying to the question Marcia seemed to have forgotten she had asked. She had finished eating and was studying her fingernails, intent on some flaws in their vermilion varnish. 'I booked her on the midday flight from Johannesburg.'

'Well – I'll be at the bridge club. It's the weekly pairs competition.'

'Don't worry, Marce. I'll fetch her. I've cancelled some appointments.'

The plane arrived on time, thank goodness. Alec had an apisectomy scheduled for two thirty and it would have put his appointment system out completely if his mother had been late. As it was, he had cancelled three patients to make space to meet her. Why was she always the last passenger to emerge? Alec peered and fretted and frowned and failed to find Zelda among the arrivals and was suddenly worried that she'd collapsed in mid-air. His fear seemed confirmed when he finally spotted her – a tiny figure being wheeled towards him in an invalid chair.

'Mom!'

He bent down to kiss her, to comfort her, to prop her up. But she brushed him aside.

'Wait a second, Alec,' she said. 'Let me get out of this pram and we can say hello properly. Here. Help me with my parcels.'

'But . . . ?'

'Oh, don't worry about this.' She waved a careless hand at the wheelchair and white-coated attendant. 'There's nothing wrong with me – apart from old age and a few other things. But to travel like this is a trick I learnt from Bertha Markowitz – the best way, she told me. Zelda, she said, ask for a wheelchair and you'll never look back. She was right. A wonderful trip. Alec – give the man a little something for pushing me.'

He plunged a hand into his pocket for some coins, accepted her parcels with the other and at last they were leaving the terminal and heading towards the car-park. She was walking. Gripping tightly on to his arm, but walking. Perhaps she was going to be less of a liability than he had dreaded. Should he question her about her health? Ask her how she was doing? Or would that seem sort of . . . impatient, with someone so old? Yet he had to say *something*. 'Mom . . . ?'

But they'd reached the car and she was breathing in deeply with what he hoped was wonder and awe as she gazed at his new Mercedes. It gleamed, silver in the sunlight.

'*Alec,*' she exhaled. He backed off as he recognized her fury. 'Never would I have dreamt that a son of mine would buy a German motor car. Ever.'

Oh God. He'd forgotten. He'd forgotten so much.

'Sorry, Mom,' he said weakly, hardly knowing why he was apologizing. After all, what difference did it make to him or the Germans or Zelda or the Jews who'd been baked in the ovens if he, Alec Shindler, fancied riding round in a Merc? Anyway Marcia and her friends would have laughed him out of town if he'd objected. And in the end, he had to admit, Alec loved his car. Steering its wheel was like . . . riding on the crest of his favourite dream. But how could he say that?

'You don't seem to have brought much luggage,' he tried instead, glancing at her sitting tight-lipped alongside him. She muttered something that he failed to hear above the purr of the powerful engine.

'Pardon?'

'I said I always travel light. I came to this country with one suitcase, remember? How much does a person need?'

He shrugged. How much? He preferred not to discuss it.

'We've . . . um, Marcia . . . um, Rosie has prepared the spare room for you. I hope you're going to make yourself at home. Really.'

'Thank you, Alec,' she said formally. 'I do appreciate it. I'll try not to be ... too much ... trouble. One thing I've always sworn is never to be a burden on my son.'

'Oh, Mom.' The heat was suddenly unbearable. Had the air-conditioning failed? He wished they were home already, that he'd dropped her and was back in the surgery. When he wasn't there he longed for its whiteness, its clean coolness, its safety. How Alec longed ...

'Here we are.' At last, at last. 'Let me help you inside. I've asked Rosie to stay and help you settle in. Marcia will be back later and I'll be home for supper.'

'Would the madam like a cup of tea?'

She was standing in the doorway, a large black body wrapped in a pink overall with a white apron, reciting her offer in an expressionless voice. Doing as she'd been told.

'No ... thanks,' said Zelda even though she was longing for tea. She'd been sitting on the bed, her bed, one of the matching twin singles in the spacious guest suite of the fancy home of her son, and feeling sorry for herself. Never, she thought, shaking her head, *never* would she have imagined that it would have come to this. That she'd have had to ask, to beg almost, for Alec to take her in. And for no one to welcome her properly. Just the servant – offering her tea because she'd been told to. And look at her face. As sulky as they came. No. Zelda decided she'd rather dry up and crumble into dust before she accepted the tea.

Not that she believed people should go around pitying themselves. Oh no. She hadn't got where she was by sitting round and thinking what a terrible time she was having. She'd made the best of things.

'You're lucky, my Zeldinke,' her Mama had said when she'd kissed her goodbye and packed her off, a girl of seventeen, thousands of miles away to the cousins in South Africa. 'You're getting a chance to go to the *goldene medina* – the land of money and sunshine. We're too old to start a new life. But you – you're my baby – and you must have your opportunity.'

She remembered fighting against tears (for Zelda never cried – hardly ever) and waving to them. Waving and waving as the train pulled her away from the station platform. That was the last time she'd seen them. Her mother and three sisters and two brothers. All dead. Those spared by the pogroms had been finished off by the Germans. She had faint memories of most of them – except, of course, poor Papa, for he'd died even before Zelda had been born. At least his had been a natural death, as Mama always said. One of the few natural deaths in the family.

Zelda had left them all, carrying a single suitcase and a head full of memories – and a picture. A family photograph. Mama had seen to it that she'd packed the photograph and Zelda had kept it with her always and now she'd brought it to her son. She had swallowed her pride for that picture. Would he want it? Would he at least let her tell him about it? Zelda couldn't help a rather rueful laugh, as she propped it on her bedside table and looked at it and saw how small and dull it was. Then she sighed heavily.

'Is the madam all right?'

Rosie was still standing there, blocking the light from the passage. Why didn't she go away, to the kitchen, to her room? Who had invited her to remain here, hovering over Zelda like a black cloud?

'Fine, thank you. You can go now.'

But instead of backing out, she was entering further into the room and heading towards the adjoining bathroom and then stopping to point out something above the light-switch. Zelda saw a white button on the wall. 'There, madam,' Rosie was saying. 'The master has made a bell and it rings in my room. If you want me.'

'Yes.' What else could she say? She turned her head away to avoid the smell of Rosie's closeness and waited for the servant to leave. Rosie paused for a moment, then shook her head slowly. At last Zelda heard receding footsteps and the shutting of the kitchen door.

Alec had forgotten about his mother's insistence on a kosher diet. Another black mark. He'd forgotten, and Marcia maintained that she had never known.

'Nothing to do with me,' she shrugged, intently separating a thick spine of yellow fat from the length of her grilled chop while Alec tried to apologize to Zelda, who kept saying it didn't matter, she wasn't hungry, she would be quite happy just to have a little salad, she loved salad anyway – and wasn't it supposed to be healthier than fatty meat? Her chop lay untouched on her plate and Alec had quite lost his appetite for his.

'Mom, I promise, from tomorrow we'll organize things properly. Won't we, Marce?'

'Surely you're not expecting me to turn the whole kitchen upside down?'

Marcia paused in her final assault on the bone. She put it down and drew breath deeply. 'Sorry, Zelda – it's not that I'm trying to be difficult – but that would involve a helluva lot of upheaval, you know.'

Alec looked from Marcia to Zelda and back to Marcia again, not knowing what to say, until his mother interrupted.

'You don't have to change a thing,' she told her daughter-in-law. 'I'm quite happy to eat fish and eggs and vegetables. If that's possible.'

'Of course, Mom,' said Alec hastily. 'The easiest thing in the world.'

There was another silence until he muttered, 'Well, that's settled then,' in a decisive sort of way and Marcia rang the dinner-bell and Rosie appeared to collect the plates. The meal had been endless and unsatisfying. Alec stood up, still hungry, and walked round the table to help his mother to her feet.

'What would you like to do now, Mom?' he asked.

'I think I want to go to bed. I'm very tired. It's been a long day. Come, Alec. Come with me to the . . . my . . . room.'

He took her arm. Marcia called out a careless 'G'night, Zelda' and looked at Alec meaningfully, saying, 'Don't be long Al baby,' and he felt a thrill of anticipation as he thought maybe, *maybe* she'd feel like it tonight and tried to steer his mother quickly up the passage. But *God* she was slow. One foot carefully in front of the other. So painfully slow. At last they were in her room and he bent down to kiss her, saying goodnight as he did so and thinking hotly of his wife.

'Alec.' Zelda had her hands on his stooped shoulders and was gripping him tightly. Her fingers were surprisingly strong. He felt himself becoming limp, melting under her mother-clutch and thought of an awful joke told to him by a patient that afternoon, something about the difference between a Rottweiler dog and a Jewish mother. 'D'you know what it is?' Saul Epstein had asked in a bantering voice, his mouth full of dental apparatus. 'The Rottweiler eventually lets go.' Oh yeah? Alec had laughed bitterly. Now he stood up sharply, forcing his mother to release her hold.

'Stay a little and talk,' she was saying. 'There's so much news to catch up with.'

He hesitated. Marcia had said, 'Don't be long.' Would she wait?

'Well – for a few minutes,' he conceded. 'You need to have an early night.'

She patted the space next to her on the bed and he found himself sitting directly opposite a picture in a dull silver frame. A sepia-toned photograph with faces staring back at him – accusingly? Alec turned away. He knew that picture. He had recognized it instantly, even though he had avoided looking at it for as long as he could remember. There was something deeply disturbing about its insistent familiarity. Alec shuddered.

'Remember?' she asked softly. 'Remember how we used to look at the photo together? Me and you?'

'Yes. Of course I do.' He tried to stand up, to withdraw. But the picture seemed to demand his attention. Unable to move, he sat on the bed, close to his mother, almost on her lap again; she and he, dissolving into a warm pool of togetherness. A pool only big enough to hold small Alec and his mother – and the death-picture. Yes, that was it. Wasn't that what she had called it?

'Look at them all, my baby,' she had said mournfully. 'They're all dead now. Every single one.'

Alec had always suspected that this wasn't the entire story of his mother's picture, but hadn't wanted to know the rest. He still didn't. Looking at it had suffocated him. Made him sick. And yet, and yet – it had been so good in that velvety warmth. Nothing since had quite matched up to it . . .

'Can you still say their names?' she was asking now. Her voice had reverted to the sweet sing-song of his childhood. In a trance, he recited them. 'That's right,' she whispered encouragingly. 'Good boy.' He reached the end and there was silence and he felt her hand stroking his cheek.

'And now, Alec,' she whispered, 'I want to tell you all about this picture. I want you should know. Yes?'

'All right then. Tell me. Tell me about it, Mom.'

He had ceased being a fifty-four-year-old dentist with a silver Merc and two servants and a wife with the best figure in town. He was five again – little Alec, who wanted closeness with his mother more than anything else in the world.

She held him tightly and started talking about what a brave, clever woman her own mother had been, that even he, her

Alec, didn't have a mother cleverer than the one she'd had. And Alec listened, entranced, his eyes fixed on the solemn row of faces in her picture, on the top-hatted patriarch in a dark suit, his wife in a prim dress with a high collar, his grandfather, his grandmother. All the while, Zelda's words flowed like soft sweet treacle and he swallowed them blissfully and was soothed into a state of drowsy contentment. 'Mama was pregnant when this picture was taken, my Alec,' she was saying. 'Pregnant with me. That's why you can't see me here with my brothers and sisters.' Alec nodded, half smiling, his heavy eyes about to shut.

But then, suddenly, came a shrill cry from another world. He sat up sharply. It was Marcia. She was calling him.

'Alec! Where the hell are you? I'm not going to wait for ever, you know.'

A pain shot through his head and the smell of Zelda's lavender scent mixed with half-digested lamb chop and half-ingested mother-love suddenly made him want to gag. 'I have to go,' he said, rising unsteadily to his feet and turning away from the picture, which had become a dizzying blur. 'You can tell me . . . the rest . . . another time.'

He felt her eyes following him as he left the room and imagined their bewilderment and wondered if they were filling with tears. She probably knew, just as Alec did, that there wouldn't be another time. The moment had passed.

'She's a tough cookie, my mother,' he announced to Marcia, having squared his shoulders and blinked and swallowed and entered the bedroom with the jauntiest swagger he could manage. Alec yawned and stretched and scratched his chest and looked lustfully at his wife's naked tanned body and approached her tentatively and she allowed him to nuzzle against her. And the feel of her nipples pushed his nausea and his mother and that creepy old picture right out of his mind.

'D'you want to hear the funniest joke? Saul Epstein told it to me at the surgery today,' he murmured as he nibbled her ear. It was delicious.

'Go on then,' said Marcia, pressing against him.

Ah yes. *This* was more like it. He'd tell her the punchline and she'd shriek with laughter and say he was adorable and nothing would matter any more.

Zelda hadn't cried as she'd watched her son leaving the room. She had known that he would never be back to hear the end of her story, but she had held back her tears. Again. God knows why she'd come here to be reduced to almost-tears at least twice on her very first day. She heard raucous laughter from the master-bedroom and the rhythmic creaking of springs and then silence. Other laughter drifted in through the open window from the direction of Rosie's quarters in the back garden. Laughter peppered with exclamations in a familiar-sounding tongue that Zelda would never understand. She had come to believe that there was very little she did understand. Only the picture, and that too had lost its clarity. Even photographs faded with time.

She caught sight of herself in the small mirror on the dressing-table and moved closer and saw how lined and grey she was. Her eyes were no longer blue. Only she knew how blue they'd once been and no camera had ever captured their shade.

Long ago Eddie Shindler had gazed into those eyes and married her and given her Alec and then dropped dead after a couple of years. She had no photograph of Eddie. What shade of brown had his eyes been? And Alec's? They had always been greyish. Had they changed? Zelda sank into bed and thought how hard it was to imagine the faces of one's nearest and dearest. That was why Mama had been so wise to arrange that photograph. Or so Zelda had always believed. Now she wasn't sure.

Alec had decided to give Rosie a larger than usual bonus for Christmas. Her work-load, after all, had increased.

'Here, Rosie,' he said, handing her the envelope. 'This is for you. For the season. For the kids.'

'Thank you, master.'

She kept her eyes politely downcast as she accepted the gift and slipped it in her pocket and resumed ironing. But he remained there, hesitating, and she looked up enquiringly.

'Rosie – I'm sorry you can't be going . . . home . . . this Christmas. This year is . . . difficult, with my mother here. You understand? I'm sure by next year . . .'

'Yes – it's OK, master. I'll come back here straight after church and stay with the old madam. Don't worry.' She focused all her attention on the collar of the shirt she was pressing and finally he left the kitchen, feeling decidedly uneasy. She didn't seem happy. Yet what else was he to have done?

'Christmas is *my* holiday, Alec,' Marcia had whined. 'After all, you people have your Jewish thingies every second week. Really and truly, going out for a barbecue on the beach with the Smuts isn't a lot to ask – it's not that I'm insisting on turkey and pudding and stuff. Just a few gifts all round and a bit of booze and fun. I'm sure you can persuade Rosie to keep an eye on your mom. Listen – give her a few bob and she'll do it. Money never fails to talk to that girl.'

'You were right, Marce,' he said to her now, returning to the living-room, where his wife was stretched on a sofa, leafing languidly through a magazine. 'About the money. For Rosie. Christmas day, remember? You can tell the Smuts we're on. You won't mind, will you, Mom? We'll try not to be out too late.'

Zelda was seated in an armchair, staring vacantly ahead. She nodded. 'Have a good time, Alec. Both of you – enjoy yourselves.'

Alec smiled and congratulated himself on his skilful diplo-

macy. It was all working out amazingly well, wasn't it? He'd
been silly to have had such doubts. Weren't they three adults,
after all? And Rosie, naturally. Three adults and Rosie.

'Who is it? What do you want?'

Zelda had been fast asleep when Rosie, in her festive finery,
had returned home after the church service and peeped into her
room and noticed that the picture – the photograph she'd seen
the old lady looking at so often – had toppled over and was lying
face down on the bedside table. Rosie, having a strong sense of
order, had crept across the room and bent down to pick it up.
Carefully. So careful not to wake her. But Zelda had sensed her
presence and woken with a fright, sitting up sharply, eyes
hunted.

'It's all right, madam. It's only me. Rosie. Straightening
your picture.'

'Who? What?' Zelda, confused, was sure she'd lost her mind.
Where was she? And who was this dark figure in red towering
over her? Was she dying? Dead? Maybe already in the other
world (God forbid)? Then she heard the stranger say 'Rosie'
and looked up at her familiar face and smiled with weak relief
and said, 'Funny, I thought you were a person,' and then
realized what she had said and was ashamed.

'I mean . . .' What *had* she meant? 'It's just that I'm not used
to seeing you without your overall and apron. That's all.'

And Rosie laughed. Maybe she hadn't heard, or didn't
understand, or understood too well. Several times during the
past three weeks, while Rosie was silently tending to her needs,
Zelda had suspected that the black woman understood
everything.

'Don't worry, madam,' she was saying in her deep, evenly
modulated voice. 'Sometimes when I see myself in the mirror I

get a fright too. And my eyes grow so big and wide – almost like I'd seen the tokolosh – the evil spirit. Something like . . . those people in madam's picture.'

Rosie was pointing to the staring subjects of Zelda's photograph, which she'd carefully set right on the table. Zelda frowned. She objected to this stranger making reference to her picture. It was her legacy, her talisman, her heritage. Her son's heritage, whether he liked it or not.

'Don't . . .' she began and then caught herself. What did it matter? 'You look very smart, Rosie,' she said instead. 'They told me you'd been to church.'

Rosie nodded. 'It's Christmas, madam.'

As though Zelda didn't know. Did Rosie think she was living in a different world? Perhaps she was. Zelda glanced at her picture and imagined a brief flash of faraway frozen light. She hadn't been part of that world either.

'There's a better world to come, God willing,' she muttered to herself.

Since that night, the night she'd almost told Alec the story of her picture, Zelda was often saying things to herself. No one seemed to take much notice. At meal-times they brought her fish and eggs and vegetables and Marcia complained about the heat and Alec talked about the money-markets and each night he asked without fail, 'Everything all right, Mom?' and she said, 'Yes, of course. Why shouldn't it be?' and he took her to the bedroom. They'd never spoken after the first night. Not about anything that mattered.

Rosie was still looking at the picture. Shaking her head and frowning.

'You have a son, don't you, Rosie?' The question had come out involuntarily.

'Oh yes, madam.' Rosie moved to the window and smiled at the garden with its sun-scorched succulents and the pampas grass that rustled in the early afternoon breeze. 'I have a boy. A beautiful clever boy. He was seven last October. Maybe next month I'll see him again.'

She turned round to Zelda, who'd propped herself up on the bed. Their eyes met. 'It's hard to be a mother, madam. Very hard.'

And Zelda nodded. 'Rosie . . .' She hesitated. 'Come here. I want to tell you something. About my . . . this photograph.'

Slowly, very slowly, Rosie came to the bed and crouched down to study the picture. Zelda took a deep breath and was about to begin. But then a long, low whistle pierced the silence and Rosie jumped up and strode across the room to the open window.

'Johnson!' she called out joyfully. 'Hey! I'm here.'

She turned to Zelda. 'Madam,' she began. But Zelda was tired. Exhausted. Barely able to hear the servant's excited babble about a Christmas party that she and the gardener had organized. 'Just a small party, madam. In my room. It will be very quiet – no trouble. And – madam. If you want me you must press the bell. I'll come straight away. It's a promise. OK?'

Zelda nodded weakly.

'And madam – God's my witness that this is going to be the last party. Just for Christmas. After today, madam, it's finished with beer and fahfee and everything. And – *madam*.' She bent down close to Zelda, who had shut her eyes. 'Will you tell me about your picture tomorrow?'

Zelda mumbled something and lay quite still until the echo of the exultant 'See you later, madam' had completely died away. Rosie could never have understood the story anyway, she decided. Neither understood nor believed it. A death-picture? Zelda would never have believed it herself if she hadn't known that her Mama would never, ever have told her a lie. 'Without this picture, Zeldinke,' she'd said, 'you'd never have known what your Papa looked like.'

'Why, Mama? How come?' Zelda had asked. 'What do you mean?'

'I was pregnant with you when he died, remember,' Mama had explained. 'He died suddenly – and the first thing I thought (I was very upset, naturally) was that my baby, my sixth child who was yet to be born, would never know its father.

'So, before we did anything else, I called your brother Itzik and I said to him quickly he must fetch Yankel Fleishman, the photographer. "But, Mama," he said, "what about the burial society? The rabbi?" "Itzik," I said firmly, "I'm your Mama and I'm telling you to go and bring Yankel. The picture comes first."

'Quickly we put Papa into his best suit – everyone had to help. Papa wasn't a small man and dead he was no lightweight. Then we dressed up ourselves. It was an important day. And by the time Itzik had come back with Yankel, we had your Papa lying on his back on the floor looking very smart indeed.

'"Now, this is what I want," I said and gave Yankel his instructions – it was the first death-picture he'd ever taken, you see. And I showed everyone in the family how to lie on their back next to Papa. All of us in a row. And Yankel stood over us and his camera flashed. Once, twice – just to make sure. "Hold still – don't move!" he ordered everyone – except of course poor Papa. Afterwards we closed your father's eyes. The next day he was buried.'

Zelda had taken the picture and the empty, dead eyes of her Papa had looked at her and she'd sworn she'd never forget him. And now (still remembering, forever remembering) Zelda tried to shut out the noise drifting in through her window. Sounds of life, vibrant voices coming from Rosie's room. 'Silent night' being sung with drunken glee.

At last she slept with the carol splashing into her ears.

Darkness fell and Zelda slept on, unaware of the shouts and songs and sounds of celebration until they turned to cries that startled her awake. A police siren screeched through the un-silent night. Then an engine roared and stopped with a squeak of tyres followed by loud footsteps and banging doors and harsh commands. And then the night was still. Calm and quiet.

The following morning Zelda told Alec and Marcia that she'd decided it would be best if they found her a place in a home. They didn't argue. Alec was nursing a hangover and Marcia was worrying about a replacement for Rosie who, just as she'd predicted, had come to no good.

Luckily, there was a gap in Alec's diary on the day his mother was booked to leave. The usual January flurry of cracked crowns and lost fillings had not yet begun, for his patients tended to deal with post-festive depression and digestive dis-orders before they got round to their dental disasters.

'Are you sure about this, Mom?' he asked tentatively as they left for the airport. Marcia had said a distracted goodbye to her mother-in-law before setting off for the club. It was the monthly women's pairs competition and that always made her nervous.

'Yes, Alec. You mustn't worry about me,' Zelda said firmly, looking straight ahead. He wondered if she meant it, then noticed the dust on the bonnet of the car and thought he'd ask Johnson to polish it and then remembered that Johnson as well as Rosie had been arrested on Christmas night. What a disaster that had been. Marcia disappearing for hours into the sand-dunes with Bokkie Smuts, he consoling himself with brandy and Coke and getting sick – and then coming home to find the police had raided the servants' quarters. Thank God his mother hadn't woken. Slept like a top all the way through – but then announced the next day she was leaving. Most strange.

After everything that had been done for her, as well. Who knew what went on in old people's minds? Alec pressed his foot on the accelerator. The car surged forward and Zelda grabbed the dashboard.

'What's the rush, Alec? You're in a hurry to get rid of me?'

He slowed down, laughing uncomfortably.

'Sorry, Mom. Of course not.'

Not much was said after that. He helped Zelda with her luggage (which seemed to be even lighter than when she'd arrived) to the check-in counter and she insisted on walking to the plane.

'But, Mom – you told me that a wheelchair was the best way to travel. Let me organize one for you.'

'Leave it alone, Alec,' she said in a voice that brooked no argument. 'I can't be bothered with that sort of thing any more.'

He couldn't bear to watch her halting progress across the tarmac. Instead, he tried to think about his appointment schedule that afternoon and the yacht he was planning to buy and whether, if Marcia did well in her bridge competition, she'd be in a good mood that night. Alec waved and smiled at his mother, who paused at the top of the steps before disappearing into the plane.

'*Marce,*' he said enthusiastically a couple of weeks later, 'I must tell you that the steak's delicious. This new girl of ours is turning out to be outstanding.'

Marcia smiled, gratified. Luring Beatrice from the Oppermans had been worth it. Who knew when that Rosie would get out of jail? Found guilty of dealing in illicit liquor, gambling, prostitution – hell, she'd probably be there for life.

'By the way, Al,' she said, fiddling with a lettuce leaf, 'Beatrice was cleaning out the spare room yesterday and she found that old photograph – you know, the one your mother kept next to her bed when she stayed here? It was under the bed. D'you think she might have forgotten it?'

Alec shrugged.

'Maybe. What did you do with it?'

'Nothing. I told Beatrice *we* certainly didn't want it, so I suppose she threw it away or something. We *don't* want it, do we, Al?'

'No.'

Alec inserted a cube of tender char-broiled fillet into his dentally perfect mouth but suddenly, for some reason, it seemed to have lost its flavour.

'No – we don't, Marce,' he said, chewing. 'We certainly don't.'

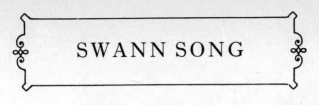

SWANN SONG

Laura Kalpakian

True, the review that ran in Friday's San Angelo *Herald* accused Jalapeño's Mexican Restaurant of Tijuana-taste in their décor, referred to their taco salad as 'an explosion in the piñata factory' and alluded to the possibility of feathers in the chicken enchilada. Moreover, the critic, Madeline Swann, had said that the names of the dishes on the menu suggested soft porn rather than soft tacos. *'Benito's Burrito? The Big Chalupa?* Spare us,' she wrote. Indeed, the only thing Madeline Swann had praised was the beer which came in a bottle. All this may have been a bit overstated perhaps, but that was the famous critic's style. Her former editor, Bert Cates, had described her column as 'cheerful hyperbole with a pinch of malice.'

'Maybe more than a pinch,' her sister conceded as they sat at their kitchen table, two plumpish women in their fifties, their bright colors contrasting with somber faces. 'But I still don't see how this review could have cost you your job. We've said worse about other restaurants.'

'I tell you, Dorothy, this review was on his desk when I walked into the office. He tucked it in the drawer, but I saw it.'

'Maybe he was jealous.'

'Of?' Monica demanded. 'Do you really think Holt Hathaway would rather be Madeline Swann than editor-in-chief of the San Angelo *Herald*?'

'I meant of our success. Didn't James Beard himself praise our column as the best in California, the whole west for that matter? And look at the awards we've won – walls of them. Nominated for the Pulitzer in criticism –'

'Please, Dorothy, don't. You're just making it harder.'

'He didn't actually fire you, Monica, he –'

'Don't be tedious. I have been fired. Just because Holt Hathaway indulges in spurious euphemism doesn't mean that we should follow suit. It impugns my integrity.' Monica Evans shook her head. 'I came to the *Herald* when a woman couldn't do anything except answer the phone or print recipes that called for canned soup or lime Jell-O. I now have the most celebrated food pages in California – better than the San Francisco and Los Angeles papers. The best.' She glanced across the table at Dorothy who was fighting tears. 'And now I'm going to lose my job.'

Monica rose and faced the kitchen window. Their house sat on a cliff of this fashionable beach town, bought many years ago when such houses were affordable. It was too big for them since Monica's youngest son had left four years before, but they stayed comfortably on. They had no ocean view, but they could hear the sea at high tide. The sound of the sea had not changed and the railroad track still cut through town like an old appendix scar on the belly of a starlet, but San Angelo now was all pastel condos and look-a-like mission prefabs. The view had certainly changed, but Monica had first been captivated by the contrapuntal collusion of train whistle, wind and sea, when, twenty-five years before, she had come here, plunked her sons and her sister down in a rented home, and gone in search of a job. She had found a life, a calling, an identity. 'I created Madeline Swann,' Monica said at last. 'Now I am being fired, and they will keep my creation, and that little fraternity brat, that illiterate meatball, Dan Drischell, will write under my name.'

'Maybe it wasn't the review,' Dorothy sniffed. 'Maybe they meant to get rid of us all along.'

'Maybe. They certainly got rid of everyone else.'

'And they promised us everything would stay the same.' Dorothy always used the editorial 'us' in speaking of the *Her-*

ald, although she was not employed there. In fact, Dorothy Culpepper was technically not employed at all – and now, for that matter, neither was Monica Evans. Hathaway had made Monica's choices clear: she could go out gracefully like Bert Cates, or take a humiliating demotion like Stan Herbert.

For more than half a century, the *Herald*, San Angelo's laconic local rag, had been owned by the Wampler family – limited, obtuse and incompetent to a man, but decent folk who demanded only that their coffee be fetched at board meetings. The Wamplers cheerfully left the running of the paper for thirty years to Bert Cates and his managing editor, Stan Herbert. Naturally, when (in the eyes of the *Herald* employees) the younger Wamplers turned spineless and greedy and sold the paper to the huge RamTec chain, Bert Cates was the first to go, prematurely and forcibly retired into an endless unsatisfying round of golf, television and a few too many drinks before dinner. Then, a few too many drinks before lunch. Bert Cates was literally of the old school. He came to the *Herald*, as did most of the old-time employees, via the student newspaper at San Angelo High School and after graduation he picked up a few units in English at the Community College before returning to the inkslinger's trade. The advanced education of Bert and people like him consisted of persistently sophisticating their powers of intuition and avoiding the word 'it'.

The RamTec people by contrast were truly and without doubt Word Processors. Holt Hathaway, BA, MA, Boy Wonder, came from a RamTec paper in Chicago trailing clouds of glory and a dozen underlings he put in strategic jobs. He was ruthless and efficient and, seemingly overnight, the old metal and ink smell of the pressroom vanished, replaced by the blip and plastic chatter of computers. Computer jockeys in Reeboks jogged in to oversee the new equipment, and the old pressmen – the ones with inky fingers and leather aprons and oil rags sprouting out of their back pockets – all those men shuffled out the back door. Some found work at the Vo Tech; some did not. In the city room, in Sports, Circulation, Classified, Living, Local, Obits, Reception and everywhere else, green computer terminals sprouted up at all the desks, and those who could not get the hang of them (and even those who could) quit, were fired, or ignominiously demoted like the former managing editor, Stan Herbert. Stan had seemingly clamped the same cigar in his teeth since 1955, camped at his desk, typing with two fingers and bullying everyone. Stan's methods were peremptory, personal, effective and hopelessly passé. Now Stan had been given the title, Legal Editor, and he wrote Obits in a broom closet, taking the information from forms filled out and left at his desk by the bereaved families. He told Monica that he had accepted this affront because 'I work, or I die. When you know that, it simplifies things.'

From all this upheaval and casualty Monica Evans had considered herself immune, a belief which time seemed to have borne out. After all, RamTec had been here for over two years and besides, Monica was much more than simply food editor. She was also Madeline Swann and her famous restaurant reviews ran every Friday. When Madeline Swann won awards, Bert Cates accepted them on her behalf to protect her identity. It was common knowledge that the San Angelo Restaurant Owners' Association had offered a bounty to the waiter who could correctly identify her. One hundred, two, five hundred dollars: it had never been collected. When Madeline Swann praised a restaurant, they framed the column and put it in the window; they copied and enlarged it and paid good money to run it again in the very pages where it had originally appeared for free. When Madeline Swann panned a place, it closed within the year. Her taste was catholic and unerring and (surprisingly, in this very rich resort town) democratic. She brought her wit, her perfect palate, her impeccable taste, her pen with its pinch of malice to Paco's Tacos as well as Il

Florentine. Snobbishly she refused to review any chain restaurant, even the best of which she dismissed as 'cardboard and candlelight'. Any independent undertaking, however, merited – or risked – her inspection. She approved the Delta salad and the Saigon coffee at the Mekong, waded through sawdust and rock and roll to praise the Hangtown fry at Bully's Beefy Ribs and zapped the artichoke soufflé at Café de Paris where the chamber trio played Vivaldi.

And no one knew who she was.

Collectively, and judging from the internal evidence in her columns (as well as a few hunches), the Restaurant Owners had compiled a profile on the mysterious Ms Swann. They reckoned her to be about thirty-five, believed she was tall and habitually dressed in smart, severe, tailored clothes, favored frosty white silk blouses, and for some reason, her prose further suggested a single, waist-length string of pearls artfully draped around manicured fingers. Her education (she obliquely gave the reading public to understand) was Bryn Mawr (Cum Laude) and her culinary tastes formed in Paris, Rome, New York and El Paso.

In truth, the svelte, sophisticated Madeline was the creation of the two sisters who were joyed-over to wear a size 14 and colored their hair at home with L'Oreal because they deserved it. Their cosmopolitan culinary tastes and elegant writing style reflected simply their native, God-given genius. They had spent their childhood in a rag-tailed Arkansas town where one could be white and poor, or black and poor, literate and poor, or illiterate and poor. The Culpepper family was white and literate and not as poor as most. The girls spent the most significant ten years of their youth in Washington, DC when their father, Judge E. C. Culpepper, became a congressman. Here the girls lived the heady lives of DC débutantes of a bygone era: cream-colored invitations pinned three-deep to the wall, twelve-button gloves for evening, three-button little white gloves for afternoon tea, dozens of doting military cadets, fawning congressional aides and law students of exceptional political promise. A life of charity balls and garden parties, of satin, chiffon, high heels, and kisses stolen in the back seat of diplomatic limousines.

Congressman Culpepper died in the middle of his third term; he had a heart attack in the Mayflower Hotel while successfully selling his vote to a female lobbyist. Humiliated and impoverished, Mrs Culpepper returned to the (paid for) Arkansas family home, taking the more compliant younger daughter, Dorothy, with her. The elder, Lillian (the Judge had a thing for the Gish girls), declared flatly and in non-negotiable terms she would never return to Arkansas. She intended that her DC life should go on for ever. Lillian promptly changed her name to Monica and married the first law student she could lay her hands on, figuring she could make a senator of Nestor Evans. Given Monica's executive abilities, her determination, her drive and quick intelligence, her genius for written expression – given that and a different climate of opportunity – Monica could have gone to law school and become a senator herself. Nestor Evans, on the other hand, like many resoundingly mediocre people, was handsome, ineffective and inoffensive, but by the time Monica finally gave up on him, she had three small sons whom she packed up one day in the asthmatic Ford station wagon. Nestor said she could not leave him. Monica replied: *Watch me*. She wired her sister Dorothy, who had never married and who had continued to live in the Arkansas house after their mother died. The telegram said: *Driving to California. Pack*. They drove until they came to the Pacific Ocean and then they turned right. They drove north to San Angelo. Then stopped.

'Maybe we could sue Holt Hathaway and the *Herald*,' Dorothy suggested.

'For bad taste?'

'For firing a woman and hiring a man.'

'A boy,' Monica said bitterly. 'No, Holt's beaten me even on that score. This morning he pulls me into his office and reads me the memo before it leaves his desk and when I start to protest, he says he isn't here to argue with me – oh no, simply to inform me that I no longer am qualified for my own job and –'

'The swine.'

'– to give me the rest of the day off. The rest of the week if I liked.'

'The rest of our lives,' Dorothy wept.

'Yes. And the way the memo is worded, I haven't a hope of recourse. Look at that.' She pushed it across the table. 'The *Herald* is smashing gender stereotypes! As of Monday! A woman, Sally Slocum – it really says that, as though with a brain to play with you wouldn't know Sally Slocum was a woman – will become sports editor! And Dan Drischell – a man! – will be the new food editor.' Monica sat down glumly. 'Affirmative action, rejoice.'

Dorothy poured them both another cup of tea. She coughed and cleared her throat. 'If you quit, we won't be able to get unemployment.'

'Now Dorothy, I thought we agreed long ago that you are the artistic one and I'm the pragmatic one.'

'Well?' Dorothy looked at her beseechingly.

'We'll hang on to the house as long as we can.' Monica rose and took her battered straw hat off the hook. 'I'm going to walk down to the beach and when I come back, I'm going to take a nap. Tonight I'll go into the *Herald*. I'll leave my letter of resignation on my desk and clear out when no one's there.'

'Clear out twenty-five years in one night!'

'Dennis will help me.'

'Even at that –'

'What choice have I? Maybe Stan can write Obits, but I could never go back to listing the engagements of local girls.'

'We're too young to retire and too old to get new jobs,' Dorothy cried. 'We're going to end up like Bert.'

'You don't end up till you're dead,' Monica replied unconvincingly. 'It's not over till then.'

By midnight, even the security guard knew of Monica Evans' dethronement. She could tell from the look on his face. 'Ring up Dennis,' she said tartly, 'and send him up to my office with some boxes.'

'How many?' asked the guard with a pinch of malice.

She took the escalator to the third floor, Features. The whole vast room was deserted, all the little green blinking eyes of computers turned off and the Muzak (another RamTec innovation, along with the guard and the escalator) clearly audible in the silence. Monica walked through the sea of desks towards her glassed-in office, beaching briefly on the shoals of Dan Drischell's desk where she gazed at the single picture. Unlike most people, whose spouses or children adorned their desks, this was a framed photo of Danny-boy himself, sporting a frat T-shirt, a squash racket and a yeasty grin. 'Figures,' she mumbled, moving on. Insult to injury to replace her with Danny Drischell – he of the MFA degree whose writing could only be described as MTV. Next week his name would be on the door and his words passing as Madeline Swann's.

At her own door Monica tried to peel off the brass nameplate (a gift from Bert), but it would not come. She glanced in at the rows of cookbooks and awards. Unsuccessfully she fought tears. Finished: the glorious fourteen-hour days, the deep satisfactions of print, the secret pleasures of being the F. Scott Fitzgerald of food writers, the Perfect Palate, the *grande dame* of entertaining in one of the richest towns on the California coast. The loss was all the more unendurable because, for a woman whose life was spent writing about entertaining, hospitality, good food, good wine, good taste and all that associated camaraderie, Madeline Swann had no friends. Monica Evans very few. A woman who works that many hours doesn't have time to cultivate friends. Society, Books, Theater, Features, Living, all those old friends and editors and writers had succumbed to the RamTec purges. Monica missed Bert the most. Monica and Bert had not only been friends, for a time they were lovers, the affair lasting eight wonderful, turbulent, fulfilling months, terminated by mutual consent when Bert's wife discovered she had cancer. His wife died painfully three years later. Monica and Bert did not resume their intimacy because Monica did not want another husband and Bert badly wanted to remarry. He did and was subsequently, shortly divorced.

Of the old guard, Stan Herbert alone remained, grown even more crusty and irascible after his demotion to Obits. But Monica was grateful that RamTec seemed to have spared the maintenance staff altogether and this allowed her to keep her friendship with the third-floor janitor, Dennis Quinton. A woman who works fourteen hours a day tends to make friends with the after-hours folks and Dennis was reliably good company – irreverent, funny, a man in his thirties who strapped his Walkman on the way a gunfighter wears a holster. Dennis's job was cleaning up, but his life, his single passion, lay in black-and-white landscape photography to which he donated his every spare dime and minute. Two of his pictures hung framed on Monica's wall. Dennis had an exaggerated love of the vernacular and when he arrived in Monica's office laden with boxes, his opening words instructed RamTec to a collective undertaking physiologically impossible.

'You've heard about the interoffice memo then,' she said.

Dennis knelt in front of the small fridge in her office where, as testament to their friendship, Monica allowed him to keep beer (forbidden in the Wamplers' day, grounds for dismissal by RamTec). He whistled *The Bridge on the River Kwai*. He got out two Budweisers and using his tank top (attire forbidden by RamTec) to get a grip on the caps, he opened them and handed one to Monica. 'The thought of Dan Drischell in this office makes me puke, but I guess only a fraternity boy can become a RamTec man.'

'Small comfort.'

Dennis flung himself down in the chair opposite her desk. He drank reflectively. 'When Drischell's first column appears, there won't be a sober waiter on the whole California coast, Monica. Champagne corks will pop in every eatery from the Savoy Grille to Kim Chee's Cabbage Palace.'

'They won't know. Drischell will keep the name, Madeline Swann.'

'Oh come on – from the lead paragraph they can tell! Drischell couldn't write his way out of a candy wrapper and besides, what he knows about food could be put in a chewable vitamin.'

'In and of itself,' Monica said slowly, 'that's not a crime. In fact – well, if you want to know the truth, Dennis – I don't know dim sum about food myself. I have ball bearings for taste buds. My idea of a good meal includes ketchup, syrup or peanut butter.' She shrugged. 'It's my sister, Dorothy. Dorothy is the cook, the gourmet, the one with the 14-karat palate, the fine eye for ambience, the elegant taste and sensibilities. To me, Beef Wellington and beef jerky are all the same.'

'You mean your sister is Madeline Swann!'

'I didn't say that. Dorothy isn't a writer. We go out and she keeps all her notes in her head, writes them up at home and then I take her notes and cook them up into savory prose. We wait ten days to run the review so no one ever guesses. It takes two of us, and aside from the fact that we can pool our gifts into one person, what waiter is going to pay any attention to a couple of middle-aged women?' She smiled ironically. 'Two women in their fifties are lucky to get a table and a refill on the coffee. People as ordinary as Dorothy and me, we're invisible. We go in, Dorothy tells me what to order; we sit there and talk about the children and the grandchildren. Just a couple of Old Girls on an evening out.'

'Son of a gun! No wonder you've survived all these years and kept them guessing!'

'Dan Drischell will probably flash his press card to get a table,' Monica added glumly.

'Will he even need a press card at Jalapeño's?'

Monica regarded him quizzically.

He grinned. 'I grant you, Monica, that dumping trash cans don't give me no MFA like little Danny Drivel, but it's an education of sorts, 'specially if you have a few brains to begin with. I was reading your column on Jalapeño's and I had this sudden – you might say – fit, a fit of *déjà vu*, sort of like indigestion. Kind of like what Hathaway has – you know, his fridge is full of Maalox and his trash can's got a lot of empty Pepto Bismol bottles.'

'I always thought that smell was his aftershave.'

'No telling what turns his wife on. But, as I was reading what you said about Jalapeño's, I got this sour little taste, right about here.' He pointed to his Adam's apple. 'And pretty soon, I burped it right up. *The Big Chalupa? Benito's Burrito?* And I remembered! I found them names – them and a lot worse – in Hathaway's trash can, oh, maybe three or four months ago now. I remember reading them and thinking – what the hell is this dude up to?'

'What do you mean, you found those names in the trash can?'

'Carmen Miranda, Monica! Use your brains! It don't take no MFA to put it together. Holt Hathaway *wrote* the names on that menu. You come down hard on the restaurant, but you stood the menu up against the wall and shot it. *Spare us!* Weren't those your very words?'

Monica dabbed the perspiration gathered at her upper lip and took a sip of beer.

'I bet you a case of Budweiser, Jalapeño's is run by Holt's relatives. Come out from Chicago and don't know salsa about Mexican food, but figured, well – what can you do to a bunch of tortilla chips?'

Monica took a few short breaths, paled and gulped. 'The owners *are* people from the East who've recently come out here. I can't remember the name. A common name.' The expression on her face began to dissolve rapidly like an Alka-Seltzer in tonic water. 'Holy frijole, Dennis! Holt. That's their name, I never –'

Dennis shook his head, rose, flipped his Bud bottle in the trash and got out two more. 'You really put your foot in it.'

'He can't do that! It's against the Constitution, somewhere.'

'He's done it.' Dennis began packing up her cookbooks and taking her awards off the wall. 'He's left you two choices. Bert or Stan. Bert's sitting in a big house massacring his brain cells with alcohol and Stan's sitting in a broom closet writing Obits.' Dennis finished filling one box and began on another. 'Don't worry about any of this, Monica. You just go on home. I'll pack it up, desk and all, and bring it by your house tomorrow in my van.'

When she did not reply, Dennis turned, surprised to see the middle-aged, chunky Monica rising from her chair with the cool aplomb, the patrician demeanor, the classic outrage of Madeline Swann, figuratively fingering the long rope of all-purpose pearls. 'It is absolutely impossible that Madeline Swann should be bested by someone who would actually dream up the name, *The Big Chalupa*,' she declared in a manner reminiscent of both Marie Antoinette and Margaret Thatcher. 'Holt Hathaway may be editor-in-chief, but he will not force Madeline Swann to lie in the same bed of lettuce with Dan Drischell!' She gave Dennis an imperial smile. 'We are not without resources.'

*

Holt Hathaway had a receding hairline, or if you prefer, a prematurely advancing forehead and what was left of his curly hair was graying so he looked older than his thirty-seven years. He was tall with a loose, unwieldy jaw and a great deep voice that echoed in his chest. He was, as Dennis had correctly observed, seriously dyspeptic and he reflexively checked for a Maalox moustache as his secretary announced that Stan Herbert was here to see him.

Stan shambled in without bothering to remove his cigar. His pot belly folded over his belt and his bald dome gleamed in the fluorescent light. Accustomed to many years of command, he immediately demanded to know why he'd been called up from Obits. 'Someone's gotta look after the dead, you know. They're a pesky bunch.' For all his years on the California coast, Stan had never entirely got West Texas out of his larynx.

'What's the meaning of this?' asked Hathaway, equally accustomed to command and rattling a paper before Stan's face.

'Looks like an Obit, only longer.'

'You wrote it!'

'I never saw that before in my life,' Stan stated flatly. 'I'm not the responsible party. No sir, not any more. The families of the dead, they fill out their forms and –'

'There isn't any family! There isn't any Madeline Swann! This Obit appears in the very same paper – the very same section – with Madeline's column!'

'With Dan Drischell's column,' Stan corrected him.

'She's reviewing the Cinquantaine Restaurant and described as dead in the same paper! How does that look?'

'I don't know. How does it look?' Stan inquired earnestly, then he turned sly and added, 'Maybe it was the food killed Madeline Swann. Maybe it was the food at Jalapeño's.'

Holt Hathaway's resident ulcer gave a particularly painful thump. His heavy jaw tightened and his eyes narrowed, but he had been an editor-in-chief since he was twenty-eight and he knew how to deal with Stan Herbert and people like him. 'There has been an error,' he said succinctly. 'You will write a retraction for tomorrow's paper. You will expose this hoax and take editorial responsibility for it. Have it on my desk in two hours.'

'All right,' said Stan resignedly. 'Let's have a look.' He picked up the paper and read slowly while the ashes from his dead cigar dribbled on the carpet.

Late of this city: Ms Madeline Swann, restaurant critic for the San Angelo Herald, renowned for her unerring taste and impeccable prose.

Ms Swann was born in Washington, DC to a very old, rich family with diplomatic connections and spent her childhood traveling to various ambassadorial posts, living in all the important capitals of Europe, Asia and the South Seas. In these early years she acquired the eclectic range of her culinary taste and the broad spectrum of her epicurian judgment.

'Whew! I see what you mean!' Stan cried. 'What self-respecting newspaperman would use a phrase like eclectic range or epicurian judgment? Whoever wrote this oughta be taken out and shot!'

'One hour and fifty-five minutes.'

Ms Swann returned to her own country at the age of eighteen to attend Bryn Mawr where she majored in Comparative Literature, aided in this venture by her mastery of five different languages. She was a member of Phi Beta Kappa, as well as Cordon Bleu, before she was twenty-one.

Ms Swann had a richly romantic personal life, including love affairs with well-known actors, an Italian industrialist, and assorted English peers. Her only husband, however, was an itinerant musician with whom she eloped, leaving Bryn

*Mawr behind for ever to wander the West in a pickup truck.
He played a heartbreaking alto sax in lonely bars on wind-
swept prairies and honky tonks in mining towns. He played
melody to the desert wind, accompanied the moaning pines of
Wyoming, counterpointed the eagle's cry across Montana.
They slept in their camper and bathed in the wild rivers of
this vast country. They cooked over low open fires in full view
of No Trespassing signs. In this fashion, Ms Swann acquired
her knowledge of American cuisine. What other food critic
can claim to have made ice cream from virgin snow in the
Grand Tetons? Or say she learned her cornbread and chili
technique with a single Dutch oven and a New Mexico
sunset? Or peeled the avocados and oranges for her famous
Swann salad freshly stolen from California groves? Who else
learned the elements of fish cookery on a blue-grey island in
the Puget Sound, a just-caught salmon smoking over an
alderwood fire?*

*During this period of her life, Ms Swann made the funda-
mental discoveries which subsequently guided her distinguished life: great sex is like great food – they both require
time, imagination, energy, and a willingness to experiment.
The musician, according to Ms Swann, had a broad chest
with a thick mat of dark hair and a kiss that kicked like a Colt
repeater.*

'Why, Hathaway – this is trash! This is the stuff of cheap
novels!'
Holt glanced at his watch. 'One hour and forty-five minutes.'

*At the sweet-and-sour end of this marriage, Ms Swann
returned briefly to Europe, via New York and El Paso, but
her fortunes soon took a terrible plunge and at the lowest ebb
of her exciting life, she came to the San Angelo* Herald.
She was in the lobby filling out a job application for the

typing pool. She wore a trim blue suit, red stockings, red pumps, a silk scarf and a long rope of pearls. The Herald's *then-Editor-in-Chief, Robert Cates, passed by, struck by her long supple legs, the way they moved back and forth, as though keeping time to some complicated personal rhythm. Mr Cates was a man of sophisticated intuition and realized immediately that here was no ordinary mortal.*

Ms Swann was spared the typing pool and went to work as assistant to Mrs Millie Askew, then-Editor of the Women's Pages. Ms Swann's job consisted of dummying up announcements of the engagements of local girls and recipes that called for canned mushroom soup and lime Jell-O. Occasionally together.

Such concoctions of course were an affront to Ms Swann's distinguished palate. Sources close to the Herald *have confirmed that Ms Swann once made up one of these published recipes and took it in to Mr Cates. She put it on his desk and insisted that he eat it. It was called Broccoli Supreme, but it tasted like shit.*

'Shit! Shit? You can't use a word like that in a family newspaper, Hathaway! Don't you know anything about this business?'

'One hour and forty minutes.'

From that day forward, neither Broccoli Supreme nor anything remotely like it has appeared in these pages. Madeline Swann went on to become the region's foremost food critic, the only food critic nominated for the Pulitzer Prize.

Ms Swann died of natural causes in the service of the Herald, *choked to death on a bone thrown her by entrenched mediocrity. She leaves a grieved and bereaving live-in lover fifteen years her junior and three illegitimate children, all of whom she raised on her own glorious cooking and who are all Yale graduates.*

In lieu of flowers or donations, the family requests that remembrance be made in the form of subscriptions to the San Angelo Reveille, *Box 12345, San Angelo, California. The* Reveille *is the country's wake-up call.*

'And hour and a half,' said Holt crisply.

'Well, I don't reckon it will take me that long to write a pissy little one-line retraction.' Stan rubbed his five o'clock shadow. 'Something along the lines of – we take it all back. Madeline Swann did not die of natural causes. She slit her own wrists and took a bunch of downers, turned on the gas and hung herself when she found out that peabrain Dan Drischell –'

'I'll write the retraction myself. Get out. You're fired.'

'Thank you.'

Bert Cates pointed his lawn chair in a westerly direction and held his glass up before his face, squinting into its amber glow, the ice cubes breaking the sunset into melded elements of bronze and copper with a pale fusion of peach. The peach made him think of Monica Evans' skin one afternoon, the two of them on a sailboat, bobbing on the blue web of sea, in view of the San Angelo coastline, seeing the familiar from a whole new perspective: loving Monica was like that. The phone rang and when it did not stop, he muttered under his breath, rose and opened the screen door, padding into his kitchen. The phone continued to ring unmercifully as he refreshed his glass from the bottle of Wild Turkey on the counter. He splashed a few ice cubes in and carefully mopped up the drops on the counter. Even drunk, he was a meticulous man. He took a sip before he finally lifted the receiver and said, as he had for more than thirty years: 'Cates here.'

[163]

'Time to sober up, Bert.'

'What?'

'I'll be there in half an hour. I'm taking you to a meeting. Put down the sauce and get ready.'

'Who is this?'

'Lillian Gish.'

'Who? What do you want?'

'Don't you read the papers, Bert? This is your wake-up call.'

The offices of the San Angelo *Reveille* were not in San Angelo proper. Too expensive. Rent was lower in the nearby county town of Esperanza Point where the *Reveille* offices were wedged between a bicycle shop and Alfredo's Mexican restaurant, one of the few Mexican restaurants actually owned by a Mexican-American. The *Reveille* premises had formerly been an adult video store where you could not only rent videos, but watch them in tiny darkened cubicles. A good many bewildered derelicts often wandered into the *Reveille* offices, surprised to see Winslow Homer prints on the partition wall instead of oversize girlie photos and a petite white-haired receptionist at the desk instead of the usual bouncer. Sometimes Mrs Millie Askew could not convince these men that the adult video store was no longer and they barged through the partition, certain that on the other side, bodies yet writhed, tongues yet lolled and the endless orgasm went on and on. They were not only disappointed, but dumbstruck, some unto tears, to discover a large room full of plain used desks, noisy clanking typewriters, ringing phones, squealing chairs, active people, urgent voices. One of these stubble-cheeked winos had to be physically restrained from opening the door beneath a red light where Dennis Quinton, the *Reveille*'s photographer, was developing pictures in their dark-room.

The *Reveille* had been undertaken with the courage and conviction, the lives, fortunes and sacred honor of the principal editors, as well as business loans ballasted with the equity in their homes and, it must be added, contributions from a few of the elder Wamplers who had been dismayed by the sellout to RamTec in the first place. The costs of rent, phone, utilities, insurance and so on could not be negotiated, but salaries could and so many of the principals, people with thirty years' experience in the newspaper business, worked for minimum wage and without benefits. Some, like Mrs Millie Askew, the receptionist, and Miss Dorothy Culpepper, who answered the phone for Classified, volunteered their time altogether. The masthead read like a roll-call of people purged by RamTec. The local Vo-Tech (for a reasonable fee) printed the weekly *Reveille* with the understanding that the paper would hire their young grads, people without any experience for their résumés. To this the *Reveille* consented. You did not need experience to work for the *Reveille*. You needed to work for minimum wage and minimal bennies. You needed to have a sense of humor, a flexible schedule, a good deal of energy, a touch of irreverence and a reservoir (somewhere) of unflappable poise. You needed a strong digestive tract as most employees ate at Alfredo's Mexican Restaurant next door whose business trebled.

Stan Herbert himself presented Alfredo with the first issue. Alfredo thanked him and took it back to his office to read it in a leisurely fashion. But he swore in Spanish when he turned to Features and saw the name Madeline Swann, an eyecatching headline, twenty restaurants reviewed in her pithy, pungent, unmistakable prose along with 'the only known photo of Madeline Swann', a silhouetted string of pearls artfully draped through manicured fingers. Alfredo put the *Reveille* down and ran outside and jammed his quarter in the machine and bought a copy of the *Herald*. He turned to Features and found there the usual well-placed column by Madeline Swann. Alfredo

[165]

raised his eyes to Heaven and asked, 'Why here, God? Why right next door to me? Why me?'

Why me? Holt Hathaway mixed himself a Maalox cocktail, bolted it before he unfolded the first issue of the *Reveille* and spread it across his desk. He buzzed his secretary and told her to hold all calls. Nearly six months had passed since he had fired Monica Evans and Stan Herbert, so he was not surprised to look at the masthead and see their names, nor that of Robert Cates, nor any of the other former *Herald* old guard, whom he categorically considered malcontents, misfits and nostalgia fodder. He was surprised however to see the name of the former janitor as staff photographer, particularly since the photos were rather good, at least they were OK. He began to read and snickered: predictable pap, all of it, beginning with the editorial:

> *The* Reveille *is San Angelo's Weekly Wake-Up Call. Its conscience. Its spirit. If it touches your life, you'll find it here. If you don't, call*
> *67A-WAKE*

Everything tediously local. From sports and the splashy advertising of galleries and boutiques, from the opulent charity functions to the classifieds which promised that lost and found ads would always be run for free. They even included a picture of a lost puppy. Beneath contempt.

Holt lingered here, savoring his own superiority until at last he turned to Features with the all-but-whispered words, *be still my peptic ulcer*. There it was. The spurious photo of the string of pearls and the banner headline:

MADELINE SWANN RETURNS FROM THE GRAVE PREPARED TO TELL ALL

THE FOOD IN HEAVEN – THE FOOD IN HELL

Below were listed ten county restaurants under Heaven (complete with cherubs and musical angels) and ten under Hell (complete with flames and little devils). *Jalapeño's* led this list. Holt groaned audibly, buzzed his secretary and told her to send up Dan Drischell.

Alfredo stood squarely before Mrs Millie Askew clutching the same paper Holt Hathaway had read. He asked to speak to Miss Swann.

'She's busy.'

'Shredding reputations?'

'I beg your pardon?'

'Look. Maybe I could speak with her superior.'

'No one is superior to Miss Swann,' Millie retorted.

Alfredo nodded. 'OK. Look. I need to talk with the Main Vein. The Big Chalupa. Got it?'

Mrs Askew suggested that her assistant (Jennifer, a Vo-Tech grad with a miniskirt and a tiny gold stud punched in her nose) show Mr Torres back to Bert Cates. Bert's old sign – *Editor-in-Chief and Meanest Sonofabitch in Any Hundred Miles* – sat on his desk. The desk was compulsively neat and when he took off his reading glasses, his eyes were compulsively blue; his fair skin was no longer flushed and his hand did not tremble. Bert was not an altogether new man, but he certainly was a reasonable facsimile of the old one.

'Look,' said Alfredo, palms out in resignation, 'so, the county health inspector gives a B rating the last time she comes through. So, I water down the beans and flour up the meat a little. So, I use two eggs in the three-egg omelette and I keep

[167]

the chili relleños frozen and microwave them. So, the house wine tastes like –' Alfredo made a face,

'Bactine?' offered Bert.

'That ain't my fault. Minetti makes the wine. I only buy it. It ain't my fault.'

'So?'

'Don't sic Madeline Swann on me. Please.'

'Ms Swann chooses her own –'

'I got eyes. I can read. I know where the real Madeline Swann works. Look – here's a deal. Ten per cent. Ten per cent off for every *Reveille* employee, OK, you win! Fifteen per cent off for all your employees, only keep Madeline Swann off my –'

'Jennifer!' Bert hit the loudspeaker button on his phone. 'Would you please come back and collect Mr Torres? I think he's trying to bribe me.'

Dan Drischell's love life had improved since he became Madeline Swann. Any number of young women were eager to dine at the city's finest restaurants and (predictably) those were the only places Dan ever reviewed. He knew how to order wine and he enjoyed (at $65 a bottle) swirling it around on his educated tongue and pronouncing his austere judgment. He enjoyed signing American Express slips for meals that cost more than the weekly take-home pay of the waiter who served him. The girls ate it up and when he'd spent that much on dinner (never mind the *Herald* paid) there wasn't a woman alive who could resist him.

The appearance of Madeline Swann in the pages of the *Reveille* did not bother Dan in the least. 'Listen,' he'd said to Holt on the occasion of the *Reveille*'s first issue, 'everyone knows that the real Madeline Swann isn't going to write for some penny ante weekly printed by the Vo-Tech and written by drop-outs from the community college English Department.' Holt had his doubts, but Dan banished them. They concocted a plan where they ignored the very existence of the *Reveille*. Business as usual. Except that all calls from the San Angelo Restaurant Owners' Association got bad connections and were never returned or completed.

So it came as something of a shock to Dan to get a call early one Saturday morning, from Holt Hathaway, instructing him to be in the office in thirty minutes. Dan had to rouse his date from last night as well and, what with one thing leading to another, it was an hour and a half later that he stood, freshly showered, coiffed, laundered and unrumpled in Holt's office. On the desk were spread two newspapers: Dan's own review of the Blue Nile Restaurant and alongside it, the *Reveille*'s review of the same place. 'One of you is wrong,' said Hathaway. 'You say it's superb and Monica says camel drivers wouldn't eat at the Blue Nile. She says the food is pretentious and the prices inflated. Or vice versa.'

The two reviews lay between them like warts while Dan collected himself. 'It had to happen sooner or later,' he said.

'Would you consider three months sooner or later?'

'Be real, Holt! We're the *Herald*! They're a bunch of geriatrics and Vo-Tech types. I mean, really. Give me a break!'

'I intend to, Dan. Here it is.' Holt pushed an envelope across the desk. 'A month's closing pay and promise of a good reference from RamTec, but you're finished as food editor and you're finished in San Angelo.'

'You can't do this! I've been with you since Chicago! I've been with RamTec since I got my MFA.'

'Maybe you need a PhD,' suggested Holt.

Holt was thoroughly undone by the time Dan Drischell left his office. He took a fresh bottle of Pepto Bismol from his bottom desk drawer, cracked the seal and sniffed it, closing his eyes, bolting it down as was his custom. How could a food editor cause this much trouble? Impossible. Yet, he knew if he did not make this next phone call, RamTec would soon have him eating Broccoli Supreme. He dialed Monica's home. No answer. Of course. None of those oddballs had ever heard of the five-day work week. Saturday afternoon and they were all at the office. He dialed the *Reveille* and got their answering machine which included the blast of their name and when Jennifer's tinny little voice came on, he asked to speak to Monica Evans.

He made small talk with Monica who, for her part, flipped the loudspeaker button on her phone and so his pronouncements on the weather went all over the office. He added that she oughtn't to be working on Saturday. 'It's good of you to think of me, Holt,' she said as typewriters and voices all over the *Reveille* office fell silent.

RamTec was prepared to make her quite a terrific offer: a month's vacation and five thousand a year more than she had been making. RamTec had actually authorized Holt to go up to ten thousand, but he did not say that; he did not say that RamTec had authorized it at all. He made it sound like his own idea and not as though his Boy Wonder Butt was in the proverbial sling. 'I may have acted hastily,' he added. 'I don't think I'd truly thought out the notion of Dan Drischell as food editor. Dan's moving on.'

Stan ambled up beside Monica, took the cigar from his teeth and whispered, 'Ask him if that's like passing away.'

'Is that like passing away, Holt?'

'Ha ha ha. Well, what do you say, Monica? We're prepared to make it worth your while.'

'That's very nice of you. I'd have some conditions, of course.'

'Of course.'

'There's my sister, Dorothy.'

Over in Classified, Dorothy Culpepper rose, clasped her

hands together over her head like the Arkansas champ and got a great round of applause.

'Is there someone on the line, Monica?'

'Not that I know of.'

'What about your sister?'

'She'd have to have a job too.'

'I'm sure we could find something modest for her.'

Dorothy made a face.

'And I couldn't work without Dennis Quinton.'

'He left us without any notice.' Holt hesitated. 'But he could probably have his old job back.'

Sorting through sports shots, Dennis leaned over, practiced his gagging reflex and gave it thumbs down.

'Is there anything else, Monica?'

She ruffled her bobbed hair. 'Well, there's Stan and Bert, of course. I couldn't –'

'I'll discuss Stan with you, but Bert's out of the question. Bert's a drunk, Monica. You know that. Once a drunk, always a –'

A resounding groan filled the office and Bert was out of his chair and over at Monica's desk. He snatched the phone from her hand, but before he could say anything, she put her finger to his lips. With Holt Hathaway still squawking at the other end, she lay the phone down on the desk, took her purse out of the bottom drawer, smiled and took Bert's arm. 'Come on. I'll take you out to lunch.'

SISTER MONICA'S LAST JOURNEY

Richard Austin

When Sister Monica lay dying in a convent on the outskirts of New York, she had only one wish, apart from her desire to see God, and that was to be buried in the small village on the west coast of Ireland that had been her home. Though she had left it while still a girl, nearly seventy years ago, she spoke of it often – of the great winds rolling across the water, the hills, misty and blue in summer over which the larks climbed, the twin headlands that crouched above the sea, tawny and golden in autumn, like a great lion asleep, its head between its paws. Amid the clamour of ugly, disfigured streets in distant cities, she heard still the cawing of the rooks in bleak trees, the song of hidden birds, the angelus bell at midday that stilled the men and women working in the fields.

Sister Monica died and went to God, leaving her Sisters with her body and a considerable problem. Being so unworldly, they understood the world very well, but they had no practical experience of transporting the deceased. It was also expensive, but as she had wished it, so it must be done. They took their problem to the chapel and prayed for a considerable time, after which they decided that Sister Agnes should consult a travel agent who would put, as it were, the necessary teeth into the Lord's endeavours on their behalf. He should, for preference, be an honest man, of a seemly and discreet life, though it was not necessary that he should be a Catholic, certainly not a devout one, since they considered (quite rightly) that excessive religiosity does not always combine with hard business sense. Mr Oliver P. Wainwright of Olympus Tours seemed to be their man.

Mr Wainwright had a weakness for nuns as he had for rye whiskey, and proved to be most obliging. He struck a hard bargain, which Sister Agnes understood and appreciated, since she had no use for sentiment in purely commercial affairs, and it was arranged that the body should be flown over to Dublin by Aer Lingus and taken from thence by helicopter to its final resting place. An overdraft was bullied out of the bank manager in a matter of seconds, as he was a fearful and scrupulous man with a great terror of Hell, on which the nuns were able to play to chilling effect; a coffin was obtained, reinforced with lead, so that it might better stand the stress of travel, and this in turn was collected by an airline van and driven with haste to Kennedy Airport. God proposes, the nuns considered, but man – or, in this case, woman – disposes. They went back to their prayers, and entreated the Lord that He might give Sister Monica's remains as swift and secure a journey across the Atlantic as He had given her soul its entry to Paradise. Or so they believed, as she was a good woman who had loved God as she had her village in Ireland. She had detested America, but she never showed it.

It was at Dublin Airport the trouble began. A small helicopter had been booked by a private charter company who had quoted very reduced rates to the cunning Mr Wainwright in the hope of achieving valuable publicity from the enterprise. Although Mr Wainwright had not passed these on to his clients, he had been less than explicit to the charter company, and this provoked the misunderstanding. This was not, however, at first apparent as Sean Maguire, the managing director, led a small group of journalists to where the helicopter waited. The journalists had been well entertained, and they walked with some difficulty.

'An old lady,' Mr Maguire said with enthusiasm. 'But in touch with modern ideas, and with a modern commercial company.'

The journalists nodded, bored, sweating into their braces.

'How old?' asked one of them.

'Eighty.'

'Yes. You might have thought at her age, and a woman of great holiness, she'd have been more likely to travel on the back of an angel than be powered by Gabriel's six cylinders,' Mr Maguire said, pleased by the comparison.

'But wasn't Gabriel an angel?' asked another of the journalists. He did not care much, being a Marxist, dedicated to the overthrow of religion, but in Ireland it is difficult to distinguish after a fine lunch and a few large whiskies.

'The helicopter. That's its name. It has been blessed,' Mr Maguire said.

'By himself?'

'No, actually the bishop was not available, but he was kind enough to send a canon from the cathedral. The whole thing went off with a bang,' Mr Maguire added, permitting himself a small laugh at this touch of wit.

The group approached the helicopter, where the pilot and loaders stood together, deep in acrimonious discussion.

'Well, chaps,' Mr Maguire said, 'where is she?'

Tim O'Rorke, the pilot, nodded gloomily behind the machine. He was a thin, sandy-haired man with a tired expression and red-rimmed eyes.

'Back there,' he said. 'We're trying to winch her on.'

'What?'

'Full of lead, she is.'

The Marxist gave a small leap.

'Shot?'

'No. At least I don't think so,' O'Rorke replied. 'Unless they shoot nuns in America.'

The journalists looked from one to the other. Mr Maguire paled a fraction. O'Rorke said nothing, and began to excavate his ear with a broken matchstick.

'She's dead then?' Maguire said.

'As a dodo,' O'Rorke confirmed. 'Dead as a bag of nails, God rest her.'

Mr Maguire turned to the journalists, hands spread wide in a gesture of bewildered innocence.

'But I heard she was a pilgrim,' he said. 'They cabled from New York.'

O'Rorke shrugged.

'Pilgrim or not,' he said, 'she's certainly said her last novena.'

There was a pause.

A timid Catholic journalist, who had already written his copy and reserved the front page for a narrative of sickening piety, began to mumble a few prayers which embarrassed the others as he was already almost dead drunk and stood with great difficulty. He rocked to and fro, muttering his incantations. It seemed to Mr Maguire that no orisons had ever been born skyward on such inebriated wings.

'Arrived in a coffin, she did,' O'Rorke said. 'From New York. Dead before she started. Said so on the air way-bill. The poor creature's come here to be buried.' He paused a moment. 'The only trouble is . . .'

'Yes?' Mr Maguire said. 'Go on, man, for the love of Mike.'

'Well, she's a great weight and all,' O'Rorke said mildly. 'It's the lead coffin, I imagine, since nuns of that age are no more than a bag of bones and no mistaking. I don't think old Gabriel'll be able to take the strain.'

An uncomfortable silence fell, broken only by the scream of jets from a distant runway. A vast sense of anti-climax settled on the group, and they were uneasily aware of the presence of the dead nun in her lead coffin, of the passing of their own secret hours, one by one, towards the grave. Intimations of mortality touched each of them, as the effects of the whisky began to wear away and the sad, twilit hours of an afternoon hangover slowly emerged like a beast from its cage. One of them burped; another broke wind discreetly; the distant planes roared over the tarmac.

It was then that Mr Maguire noticed a cleric approaching them; his soutane flapped like the wings of an angry bird. He was a lean, sallow man, wearing steel-rimmed spectacles that dragged his large ears aggressively forward.

'Is Sister Monica here?' he asked in a sharp, nasal voice.

An embarrassed silence followed.

'Well,' O'Rorke said. 'She is and she isn't.'

The priest gave a small jump of irritation. 'And what exactly do you mean by that?' he said.

Mr Maguire noticed that the priest carried a large scroll in his hand, on which he caught the glimpse of illuminated lettering.

O'Rorke shrugged.

'I'm no theologian,' he said.

The priest turned to Mr Maguire. 'Are you in charge here?' he asked.

'Yes.'

'Well, do you know where Sister Monica is? I had a report from the *Catholic Gazette* about her.'

Each of the assembled journalists turned to the drunken church reporter, and glared at him. He did not, however, respond, as he had reached by now a far state of drunkenness and was, indeed, almost comatose; only the whites of his eyes showed.

'I'm afraid, Father, there's been the devil's own misunderstanding,' Mr Maguire said. 'The lady you speak of is here in a sense, but then she's dead.'

'Dead? What, just now?'

'No, Father, she arrived in that condition, one might say. In a coffin.'

For a moment the priest was nonplussed; then he thrust one great ear forward towards Mr Maguire in an attitude of ironic disbelief.

'Will you repeat that, please?' he said.

'Yes, Father. Dead. Dead as mutton, God rest her soul,' Mr Maguire said. 'We're to transport her to her village where she's to be buried. Near her home, see, as a decent woman should be when she's that dead.'

'But this is most irregular,' the priest said. 'I've been sent here by the bishop to present her with the medal Bene Merente. I don't think it can be awarded posthumously.'

Mr Maguire trembled at this. He had been an altar server in his time, and knew very well that Papal medals were not lashed around like a can of beans.

'It's a great shame, it is,' he said. 'And she being in no mood to appreciate it, if you get my meaning.'

The priest looked at him with some distaste – a curious, cold, metal-rimmed scorn in his eyes and a smile as inviting as the grille of a confessional. Mr Maguire felt he had come, earlier than usual, to his Christmas shriving, where, as a hardy annual, he was dug up and once more wearily transplanted into virtuous soil.

'Begging your reverence's pardon,' he said with an appropriate snivel.

'The bishop, of course, will have to be informed,' the priest said.

Before Mr Maguire had time to reply, Gabriel's rotor began to whir, shaking her entire structure, so that the side panels began to palpitate alarmingly like the flanks of a starving cow.

O'Rorke looked down from the cockpit.

'Shall we pull her away?' he shouted. 'I think we've got Sister Monica lashed on a treat.'

The cleric shuddered, rapping his knee with a greasy prayer book.

'Lift off,' roared Mr Maguire.

Gabriel lurched across the tarmac, skidded in a half-circle, and, with a couple of sharp explosions, slumped to a halt. The priest withdrew.

The engine blasted out again, and this time, to a spatter of grit and tar, Gabriel began to move upwards on a swinging, rather erratic course. However, the coffin did look to be well secured beneath her, and it really seemed that Sister Monica's last journey was off to a presentable start. But then Gabriel appeared to skid in the air, swung sharply downwards, scattering the watchers beneath, and landing about twenty yards from its original position. A small ooze of oil filtered from within and ran down the sides of the coffin.

O'Rorke scrambled out. He looked flushed and angry.

'It's no good, Mr Maguire,' he said. 'Because of the old lady down there, she's not properly balanced. It'd be the devil's own work to fly a straight course.'

Mr Maguire felt sick. It was not just that he would probably lose his licence, but he was most likely to be excommunicated as well. He had a vision of the grey-faced cleric clanging a great bell over his doomed head on one dark night in the empty pro-cathedral. And he'd take around the collection plate afterwards, that's for sure, Mr Maguire thought.

'What should we do?' he asked.

O'Rorke looked embarrassed.

'Well', he said, 'pardoning the familiarity, Mr Maguire, but there's only one thing to it. You'll have to come yourself. Balance the old lady. Then we'll be fine.'

Mr Maguire hesitated. It was true the idea of flying over Ireland with a coffin swinging beneath one did not exactly charm him; it was eerie, also rather discreditable. But, on the other hand, his absence from the office for a couple of days would at least lengthen the interval before his excommunication, so that perhaps the fierce cleric might begin to relent. He might indeed settle for a couple of arduous novenas, or a tramp up Croagh Patrick.

'All right,' he said. 'You're on, O'Rorke.'

I'll jump into that cockpit, he thought, as quick as an old sinner jumping out of Hell, if that's the way to escape the judgement.

He settled down beside O'Rorke as the engine began to hum.

'You see, she should have been sitting beside me now,' O'Rorke said. 'But it wouldn't be proper now, man, would it?'

He didn't wait for a reply, but allowed Gabriel, with a convulsive heave, to lift her fat body off the ground and begin her ascent. Looking down, Mr Maguire could see that the coffin swayed a little from side to side, but it seemed secure enough, though a small coil of rope was already trailing in the wind.

Soon they were high over Dublin and flying westward. The roar of the engine made conversation impossible, but, from time to time, they nodded and smiled at one another, enjoying the freedom, the cool rush of air.

The exertions of the afternoon, coupled with an extremely heavy lunch, soon proved too much for Mr Maguire. He fell asleep, mouth open, head tilted towards the sky. He dreamed of Hell, as most middle-aged Irishmen do after an indulgent midday, and he found it was a steel-rimmed pit with cold blue flames within, burning like accusing eyes. Distantly the excommunicant's bell clanged.

He woke with a start. Now they were flying over wooded countryside where already the purple shadows of evening lengthened towards the distant hills. To his left was the sea, fanning against the shore as a peacock's tail might spread itself against the darkness. He had slept a long time.

'Something woke me,' he said. 'Like a big explosion.'

O'Rorke glared at him.

'Well, it wasn't quite as loud as your snoring, I'll say that for it,' he said. 'Fit to wake the dead it was.'

At that moment there was a fierce grinding noise from the

rotor above them, followed by two loud reports and a puff of grey smoke from the axle below the blade.

'I think we're in trouble,' said O'Rorke.

The helicopter began to lose height, and O'Rorke had difficulty in controlling its direction. The grinding noise increased, and the smoke had changed in colour from grey to black; it had also thickened considerably. They began to sway around in the sky as O'Rorke fought with the controls. Mr Maguire started to pray. It's a judgement on me, he thought; in a few seconds I'll be among the goats, that's for certain, bleating my way to Hell.

The speed of their descent accelerated.

'We'll have to lose some ballast,' O'Rorke said. 'Otherwise it'll never stand the landing.'

'Ballast?'

'Sister Monica, you idiot. Cut her free.'

Maguire shuddered, rejecting the emergency saw that O'Rorke had thrust at him.

'You can't,' he said. 'It wouldn't be decent. What with her dead and all.'

'It'd be a great deal worse if she was living,' O'Rorke said. 'Then I might be after prevaricating.'

They were now about fifty feet high. After a moment's hesitation, Mr Maguire began to saw feverishly at the rope holding the coffin. As he leaned far out of the cockpit he watched the ground reeling towards them; fields and squat white cottages swerved away into the evening.

'I'll try for that field there,' O'Rorke said. 'Say your prayers, and try to bag the last few Indulgences.'

Mr Maguire now lived his own private nightmare, hacking away at the rope, seeing the ground rush up to meet him. They cannot have been more than twenty feet up when suddenly the coffin fell free, plummeted downwards, landing on the top edge and bouncing away out of sight. The speed of their descent was almost immediately eased, and they made a safe landing in the middle of a cabbage patch. Dogs barked, children shouted, and Gabriel, with a contented wheeze, settled into silence. Mr Maguire opened his eyes.

'God be praised,' he said. He made a firm purpose of amendment; in a flash abandoned billiards and porter in favour of regular rosaries and late night cocoa.

An old lady with a green shawl, three ragged children, eyes and mouths agape, a middle-aged man wearing a striped waistcoat, black trousers and slippers, stood in a dumb circle around them.

'Where is this?' asked Mr Maguire.

The little group seemed too stunned to answer. Then at last the smallest of the children, a boy of about six wearing a blue jersey full of holes, spoke for them all.

'It's Paradise, sir,' he said.

'God above us,' replied Mr Maguire. 'Now is that so?'

Dead, after all, he thought; how very odd, and no last confession either. Yet he'd made it. Why, he'd return to earth at the first opportunity, and haunt that priest with howls in the night.

'Paradise, is it?' he said. 'Well, I'll be buggered!'

The man in the waistcoat came forward cautiously, as if Maguire and O'Rorke were contaminated. A clay pipe was gripped between his teeth, and small bubbles of spittle oozed around its stem. He wore spectacles, one lens of which was cracked and the bridge protected by a wrapping of black tape; behind them his faded blue eyes peered incuriously.

'Yes, sir,' he said. 'About forty miles from Cork.'

'Oh, I see,' Mr Maguire said, disappointed, the guilt of his former sins returning in redoubled force. 'I thought you meant something different.'

The man looked at him blankly.

'Yes, sir,' he repeated. 'Near Cork, the village is.'

O'Rorke, who was paying no attention to this conversation,

looked up suddenly from his effort to tighten some screws below the rotor and shouted down at Mr Maguire.

'Where's Sister Monica?'

The spectators, who had now been augmented by some young men and two pretty girls, stirred in some alarm.

'She bounced over by those trees,' Mr Maguire said. 'I think I can see her standing on her head in the shrubbery.'

A curious murmur went around, the old lady produced a rosary from beneath her shawl and began to recite the prayers, swaying as she did so to the slow and syllabic whisper of her invocations. Heads turned in the direction of the shrubbery, anxious to see Sister Monica in her new and slightly indelicate transformation. And it was, in a sense, true, for the coffin had become upended and stood, almost upright, leaning against the branches. At this, the old lady redoubled her orisons, so that her dentures rattled devoutly together. No one moved.

'Will anyone give me a hand to shift the old lady?' Mr Maguire asked.

The children cowered away, their eyes fixed with a kind of fascinated horror on the coffin. It swayed slightly against the branches, as if Sister Monica had stirred a little within in her indignation. No one else moved; the old lady's prayers developed into a devout, jet-like whine.

'Will you be long, O'Rorke?'

O'Rorke leaned out of the cockpit. His hands were covered in oil.

'No, Mr Maguire, she's coming on a treat,' he said. 'I'm doing a fine job here and no mistake.'

Mr Maguire shrugged. He failed to see why he should congratulate O'Rorke. After all, when a goalkeeper booted the ball into his own goal, it did not seem to Mr Maguire that there was any call to praise the way he picked it out of the net. The whole stupid accident had been O'Rorke's fault, since he was supposed to supervise the checking of Gabriel before taking off; it was an elementary precaution.

Muttering to himself, he began to move towards Sister Monica's coffin which was now beginning to lurch dangerously against the trees. The last thing he wanted was for it to fall and break open, since that would undoubtedly be yet another cause in his pending excommunication. The bystanders drew aside to let him pass.

'Won't any of you help?' he asked. 'She's a fair weight, God bless her.'

The man in the striped waistcoat hesitated.

'All right, sir,' he said. 'I'll give you a hand.'

Together they lifted Sister Monica's coffin to the centre of the cabbage patch. It was cracked along the top but otherwise intact. Both stood with bowed heads beside it, as if in prayer. Mr Maguire felt that this might pacify the spectators, and give him some leeway in any subsequent action by the Church.

'Perhaps, sir, you'd like a cup of tea while your friend's fixing the motor?' the man said.

'Well, that's kind of you,' Mr Maguire said. 'I'd fancy a jar, if I might. It'd steady my nerves. I'm skinned alive like an old haddock, that I am, after this carry-on.'

Together they moved towards the house, the children and the old lady following at a safe distance.

'I'll have it fixed in a jiffy,' O'Rorke called.

Mr Maguire nodded. He was in no mood to socialize with O'Rorke whom he blamed entirely for this embarrassing situation.

While Mr Maguire and the man in the striped waistcoat drank their stout in the sitting-room, the remainder of the party and the children stood watching them, side by side along one wall, like prisoners before a firing squad. The old lady knelt at a small prie-dieu in front of a statue of the Sacred Heart, her rosary beads slipping faster and faster through her fingers as the supplications took on a greater intensity. No one spoke. It would seem that the coffin that dropped out of the air was looked upon more as a threat or an omen than as a matter of frayed rope and hydraulics.

It was obvious to Mr Maguire that they were anxious for him to be gone. The man with the striped waistcoat had removed his teeth, and these now rested on the table beside him, grinning to themselves as at some secret jest. The silence grew more intense; it frightened Mr Maguire who finished his drink in a rush, wiped his mouth with the back of his hand and stood up so abruptly that he knocked his chair on the floor.

'Well, we'd better be off,' he said. 'We've a long journey to go yet before nightfall.'

The spectators, who were still ranged against the wall, nodded in unison, but none of them spoke.

When he got outside, Mr Maguire found O'Rorke dragging the coffin towards the helicopter, struggling and cursing at the weight.

'Mr Maguire, give her a shove, will you?' he said. 'The motor's fine, and once we've got her lashed on again we can be off.'

Together they fixed the coffin to the under-belly of the helicopter. The children, the old lady, and the others stood at the back door of the cottage as if posing for a photograph. They would not approach. It almost seemed, Mr Maguire thought, as if the pair of them were contaminated.

Finally, all was in place. They scrambled into the cockpit, the engine roared, and, after a few loud explosions from within, Gabriel rose resplendent on her metal wings. Looking down, Mr Maguire saw a group of heads turned skywards, but no one waved.

'Miserable old sods,' he said.

O'Rorke swung Gabriel out towards the sea which crawled beneath them.

'It'll be best if we follow the coast,' he said.

At that moment the helicopter gave a lurch and a great leap upwards, jumping in the air like a trout from a pool. O'Rorke battled with the controls, then steadied her. They both looked down, just as Sister Monica in her coffin hit the water far below them. A great jet of spray rose; then she was gone.

'God drat it,' Mr Maguire shouted. 'Why, we've lost her for good now, you great idiot.'

They came lower and circled over the sea, where the ripples that marked Sister Monica's last resting place spread in wide rings and then subsided. There was nothing more to be done.

On the way back to Dublin Airport neither of them spoke. They were conscious of a terrible sense of failure, but, at the back of it all, there was a kind of peace. For they had completed their mission; they had buried Sister Monica, though not where she intended, but they felt certain she would rest there serenely near the village called Paradise and the waters that engulfed her would one day draw her body towards that further shore she had so greatly loved. It was dark when they arrived in Dublin.

BIOGRAPHICAL NOTES

MURIEL SPARK was born in Edinburgh and now lives in Tuscany. She is known and admired all over the world as a writer of novels and stories. Muriel Spark is also a poet, biographer and critic. Her autobiography *Curriculum Vitae* is her latest book.

PETER GOLDSWORTHY was born in 1951 in South Australia and graduated from the University of Adelaide in medicine in 1974. He is married with three children and he and his wife, also a doctor, share a medical practice in Melbourne. Peter Goldsworthy writes fiction and poetry and has been the recipient of many awards. His first novel *Maestro* was published in 1991 and he has recently finished writing his second novel.

MONICA FURLONG has worked as a journalist and radio producer, and has published three biographies of religious people – Thomas Merton, Alan Watts and Thérèse of Lisieux. She has written two adult novels, *The Cat's Eye* (1976) and *Cousins* (1983), and two novels for children, *Wise Child* (1987) and *A Year and a Day* (1990). She lives in London.

JUAN FORN is the author of the novel *Corazones Cautivos más Arriba* (1987) and the short stories *Nadar de Noche* (1991), from which the present story is drawn. Born in Buenos Aires in 1959, he has written two film scripts, one a musical for a rock group. From 1984 to 1989 he was employed by the Buenos Aires publisher Emecé as a literary editor and translator. In 1991 he became Editor-in-Chief at Editorial Planeta.

ANGELA HUTH, novelist, critic and broadcaster, has written six novels and two collections of short stories – her favourite medium, she often thinks. She was a reporter on 'Man Alive' at the BBC in the 'sixties, but since then has mostly written for television – original plays, and adaptions of her own and others' books. She has also written plays for radio and the stage. Married to a don, she lives in Oxford and has two daughters.

CHAIM POTOK was born and raised in New York City. He began to write fiction at the age of sixteen, graduated with a BA *summa cum laude* in english literature, and earned a Ph.D in philosophy. His first novel, *The Chosen*, was nominated for a National Book Award and received the Edward Lewis Wallant Award. Another of his novels, *The Primrose*, was given the Athenaeum Prize, and *The Gift of Asher Lev* won the National Jewish Book Award. His new novel, recently published, is *I am the Clay*.

WILL SELF was born in London in 1961 and educated at Oxford. He has written and cartooned for numerous publications including the New Statesman, City Limits and the Guardian. His collected cartoons were published in 1985 by Virgin Books. His debut collection of short stories *The Quantity Theory of Insanity* was published by Bloomsbury in November 1991 and his twin novellas *Cock and Bull* (also published by Bloomsbury) were visited on an unsuspecting world in October of this year.

TONY PEAKE was born in 1951 in South Africa. After graduating from Rhodes University, he moved to London, where he worked under Charles Marowitz as production manager at the Open Space Theatre. A spell on Ibiza, teaching english, history and drama, was followed by a return to London and jobs in modelling, acting and film distribution. He is now a literary agent. His first novel, *A Summer Tide*, will be published in 1993. This is the second time he has been a contributor to *Winter's Tales*.

SHELLEY WEINER was born in South Africa in 1949 and came to live in the UK in 1977. She worked as a journalist for twenty years before starting to write fiction in 1989. Her first novel, *A Sister's Tale*, was published by Constable in 1991 and was followed by *The Last Honeymoon* (Constable 1992). She lives in London with her husband and two children.

LAURA KALPAKIAN is the author of several novels and two collections of short stories, most recently, *Dark Continent and other Stories*, (Constable 1991). In 1992 Constable also published the novel *Graced Land*, the story of some California Elvis fans and how the King's energy, genius and tragedy affected their lives. Like the sisters in *Swann Song*, Ms Kalpakian likes to cook and to write. She and her two sons live on the coast of Washington State.

RICHARD AUSTIN was born in Ireland and educated at Ampleforth. He has published two novels, five collections of poetry and seven books on the ballet, including biographies of Natalia Makarova and Lynn Seymour. Many of his radio plays have been broadcast on the BBC and abroad. In 1991 he was awarded the Tom-Gallon short story prize, administered by the Society of Authors.